Birthday Stories

SELECTED AND INTRODUCED BY

Haruki Murakami

VINTAGE BOOKS
London

Published by Vintage 2006

2 4 6 8 10 9 7 5 3 1

Copyright © Haruki Murakami, 2002, 2004

'My Birthday, Your Birthday' and author introductions translated
from the Japanese by Jay Rubin: © Jay Rubin, 2004, 2006
'Birthday Girl' translated from the Japanese by Jay Rubin:
© Jay Rubin 2003, 2004

First Published with the title *Birthday Stories* by
Choukoron-Shinsha, Inc., Tokyo, 2002

First published in Great Britain in 2004 by
The Harvill Press

Vintage
Random House, 20 Vauxhall Bridge Road,
London SW1V 2SA

Random House Australia (Pty) Limited
20 Alfred Street, Milsons Point, Sydney,
New South Wales 2061, Australia

Random House New Zealand Limited
18 Poland Road, Glenfield, Auckland 10, New Zealand

Random House (Pty) Limited
Isle of Houghton, Corner of Boundary Road & Carse O'Gowrie,
Houghton, 2198, South Africa

The Random House Group Limited Reg. No. 954009
www.randomhouse.co.uk/vintage

A CIP catalogue record for this book
is available from the British Library

ISBN 9780099481553 (from Jan 2007)
ISBN 0099481553

Papers used by Random House are natural,
recyclable products made from wood grown in
sustainable forests. The manufacturing processes
conform to the environmental regulations of the
country of origin

Printed and bound in Great Britain by
Bookmarque Ltd, Croydon, Surrey

"Have a Good Time"

Yesterday it was my birthday.
I hung one more year on the line.
I should be depressed.
My life's a mess.
But I'm having a good time.

I've been loving and loving and loving.
I'm exhausted from loving so well
I should go to bed.
But a voice in my head says,
"Ah, what the hell."

Paul Simon

CONTENTS

Introduction

MY BIRTHDAY, YOUR BIRTHDAY

First, let me tell you about one particular birthday – my own.

I was given life in this world on January 12, 1949, which means I belong to the baby boom generation. The long Second World War had at last come to an end, and those who had managed to survive looked around them, took a deep breath, got married and started making children one after another. During the next four or five years, the world's population expanded – indeed, exploded in a way never seen before. I was one of the nameless, numberless children produced during that period.

Delivered in the burnt-out ruins left after the intense bombing raids, we in Japan matured with the Cold War and the period of rapid economic growth, entered the flowering of adolescence and received the baptism of late '60s counterculture. Burning with idealism, we protested against a rigid world, listened to The Doors and Jimi Hendrix (Peace!) and then, like it or not, we came to accept a real life that was neither very idealistic nor imbued with rock'n'roll. And now we are in our mid-fifties. Dramatic events occurred along the way – men on the moon, the crumbling of the Berlin Wall. These seemed like meaningful developments at the time, of course, and they may well have exerted some practical influence on my own life. Looking back now, however, I have to say in all honesty that these events do not seem to have had any special effect on the way I balance happiness vs. unhappiness or hope vs. despair in my life. However many birthdays I may have counted off, however many important events I may have witnessed or experienced first hand, I feel I have always remained the same me, I could never have been anything else.

These days when I drive my car I put silver-coloured CDs by Radiohead or Blur into the stereo. That's the kind of thing that shows me the years are passing. And now I find myself living in the twenty-first century. Whether or not the person I think of as me undergoes any essential changes, the earth never stops circling the sun at the same old speed.

In just the same way, a birthday quietly comes around for me once each year. Do these birthdays make me happy? I would have to say, "Not especially". Just turning from 53 to 54: who is going to view that as a great accomplishment? Of course, if a man's doctor tells him, "You will never live beyond the age of 52. Sorry, but you'll have to resign yourself. Now is the time to organise your possessions and write a will," and then this man greets the dawn of his 54th birthday, that is something worth celebrating. That is a great accomplishment. For that, I can see chartering a boat and setting off a massive firework display in the middle of Tokyo Bay. In my case, however, for better or worse (although, of course, it is for the better), I have never been handed such a death sentence. And so my birthday never makes me unusually happy. The most I might do is open a special bottle of wine for dinner. But let me get back to this later.

*

I myself had one very strange birthday experience – though it was strange only for me, personally.

Early one birthday morning I was listening to the radio in the kitchen of my Tokyo apartment. I usually get up early to work. I wake between four and five in the morning, make myself some coffee (my wife is still sleeping), eat a slice of toast and go to my study to begin writing. While I prepare my breakfast, I usually listen to the radio news – not by choice (there's not a lot worth hearing), but because there's not much else to do at such an early hour. That morning, as I waited for my water to boil, the newsreader was announcing a list of public events planned for the day, with details of when and where they were happening. For example, the Emperor was going to plant a ceremonial tree, or a large British passenger ship was due to dock in Yokohama, or events would be taking place throughout the country in honour of this being official chewing gum day (I know it sounds ludicrous but I am not making it up: there really is such a day).

The last item in this list of public events was an announcement of the names of famous people whose birthday fell on January 12. And there among them was my own! "Novelist Haruki Murakami today celebrates his **th birthday," the announcer said. I was only half listening,

3

but, even so, at the sound my own name I almost knocked over the hot kettle. "Whoa!" I cried aloud and looked around the room in disbelief. "So," it occurred to me a few minutes later with a pang, "my birthday is not just for me any more. Now they list it as a public event."

A public event?

Oh well, public event or not, at least at that moment some of the people throughout Japan – it was a nationwide broadcast – standing (or sitting) by their radios may have had at least some fleeting thought of me. "So, today is Haruki Murakami's birthday, eh?" Or, "Oh, wow, Haruki Murakami's ** years old now, too!" Or, "Hey, whaddya know, even guys like Haruki Murakami have birthdays!" In reality, though, how many people in Japan could have been up at this ridiculous pre-dawn hour listening to the radio news? Twenty or thirty thousand? And how many of those would know my name? Two or three thousand? I had absolutely no idea.

Statistics aside, though, I couldn't help but feel a kind of soft, natural bond with the world. It was not a bond that could serve any practical purpose, nor one that had any real impact on a person's life. It was, I suppose, that special bond that people feel with each other when they know that one of them is celebrating his or her birthday. For a while, I tried to visualise this bond in my mind's eye – its material and colour and length and angle and intensity. Again, for a time I thought about ideals and compromise, about the Cold War and Japan's economic growth. I thought, too, about growing older, and about wills and fireworks. And then I stopped thinking at all and instead concentrated on making myself a good cup of coffee.

When the coffee was ready, I poured it into a mug (one with an Australian Museum logo: something I bought in Sydney), carried it to my study, sat at my desk, switched on my Apple Mac, put a Telemann concerto for woodwinds on the stereo at low volume and started the day's work. It was still dark outside. The day was just beginning. It was a special day in the year, but at the same time it was an absolutely ordinary day. I was working at my computer. Maybe one of these years I would have the kind of dramatic birthday when I would want to sail a boat out to the middle of Tokyo Bay and set off a massive firework display. And should such a birthday ever come, I would charter the boat without hesitation, no matter what anybody might say, and I would head out to Tokyo Bay in the depths of winter with an armload of fireworks. But today, at least, was not such a day. This year's birthday was not such a birthday. I would just be sitting at my desk as always, quietly putting in a day's work.

*

As I said earlier, my birthday falls on January 12. I once looked on the Internet to see who else I shared this date with and was thrilled to find Jack London's name (and one of the Spice Girls too, I might add). I have been a devoted Jack London reader for years. Not only have I read his well-known works such as *White Fang* and *The Call of the Wild* with great enthusiasm, but also several of his lesser known stories and his biography. I love his strong, simple

5

style and his strangely clear novelistic vision, I love his singular energy, the way it transcends common sense and forges straight ahead, no matter what, as if to fill in some great emptiness. I have always thought of him as a writer who deserves far higher literary praise than he is normally accorded. To think that Jack London and I have the intimate bond of a shared birthday! His own January 12 occurred in 1876, 73 years before my own.

When I was travelling in California in early 1990, I visited the farm that Jack London owned in a place called Glen Ellen, Sonoma County, to pay my respects to this legendary writer. Or, more precisely, once, when I was making the rounds of the Napa Valley wineries in a rented car, the thought popped into my mind, "Come to think of it, Jack London had a farm around here somewhere," so I checked the guidebook and took a detour to visit the place. London bought a winery in Glen Ellen in 1905 and turned it into a large-scale experimental farm of some 1400 acres. He lived there until his death in 1916, running the farm and writing fiction. A part of his farm (about 40 acres' worth) has been preserved as Jack London State Historic Park. It's a beautiful place. The day I was there the sunlight shone with an unwavering clarity, and a quiet, pleasant breeze caressed the grass as it blew over the hills. I whiled away the autumn afternoon looking in the rooms and at the desk that London once used.

Thanks in part to such pleasant memories, I make it a point to open a bottle of Jack London wine (Cabernet Sauvignon) for dinner every year on my birthday. This particular wine is made not in Glen Ellen, but in the neighbouring district of Kenwood. Still, it is made in a winery crowned with the name "Jack London Vineyard" and its label bears the original wolf picture that was used for the cover of *White Fang*. I raise my glass in the hope that this outstanding American writer might rest in peace. This may not be the most appropriate ceremony with which to commemorate the death of a drinker of such outrageous proportions as London (he destroyed his liver and died at the age of 40). But in any case, this "Jack London" is a deliciously dry, full-bodied wine. They don't make a lot of it, so it can be hard to find, but it's the perfect accompaniment to reading London's work.

*

What originally gave me the idea of compiling an anthology of birthday stories written in English and translating them into Japanese was my consecutive reading of two outstanding stories that happened to be based on the theme of the birthday: "Timothy's Birthday" by William Trevor and "The Moor" by Russell Banks. (Of course, this is an English edition of the book, so there was no need for any translation here.) Both stories left me feeling haunted. I said to myself, "Here, I've stumbled across two great stories about birthdays. I can probably find hundreds more if I start looking for them, and if I put a bunch of them together I'll bet they would make a really interesting book. I could get an anthology's worth in no time!" If possible, I wanted to make it a book of fresh works published over the past ten or so years rather than a collection of dusty classics.

So then, day after day, I began ploughing through all the short story collections on my shelves and searching bookshops for anthologies I hadn't yet read – all the "Best of . . ." books I could find – in a single-minded hunt for birthday stories. The procedure was by no means as easy as I had assumed it would be. I was shocked and bewildered to realise that stories about a birthday could seem so numerous yet be so hard to find. Why should that be? I wondered. Could there be something innately difficult about using the subject in fiction? Or was my predicament, irrespective of theme, merely some kind of "curse of the anthologist" that overtakes all who presume to assemble a volume of related works? I had translated any number of British and American stories in the past, but this was my first attempt to edit my own anthology. Maybe I had simply not appreciated what an arduous task that can be.

Lynda Sexson's "Turning" and Raymond Carver's "The Bath" were both stories I had published before in my own Japanese translation, so all I had to do was take them from my earlier work. "A Game of Dice" featured in Paul Theroux's *Hotel Honolulu*, which I happened to be reading at the time so I decided to use that too. I came across Daniel Lyons' "The Birthday Cake" quite by chance as I was flipping through the pages of a book I had on the shelf. And a totally unrelated event reminded me that Denis Johnson's "Dundun" was another good birthday story I knew. With the Trevor and Banks stories, that made seven altogether, but the process pretty much ground to a halt after that.

I gave up hope of finding enough stories myself and started asking acquaintances for help. I phoned just about everybody I could think of to ask if they knew any recent good stories about birthdays. I was on the phone to Amanda (Binky) Urban, my agent at ICM in New York, when it occurred to me to ask her the same question. "You're in luck, Haruki," she said. "Last week's *New Yorker* had a great birthday story by Andrea Lee. I'll fax it to you." "The Birthday Present" arrived on my Tokyo office fax machine a short time later, making it by far the freshest product of the bunch. And the story itself carried a real wallop.

Neither Ethan Canin's "Angel of Mercy, Angel of Wrath" nor David Foster Wallace's "Forever Overhead" were stories I found myself. A friend alerted me to the existence of one and an editor to the other. Both were relatively new works by young authors and, though utterly different in style, both had a satisfying weight to them that immediately won me over. That made ten stories now and, though still heaving sighs with the effort, at least I had the makings of an anthology.

Finally, it occurred to me that since I had started this project, I would try writing a birthday piece myself. In the course of reading other writers' stories as editor, I had begun to feel that I wanted to try my own hand. I guess it was a case of not wanting to miss the party – even if it meant I had to crash it. Writing "Birthday Girl" was more fun than hard work for me, and I hope you will read it with the same easygoing attitude. It tells the story of a girl's lonely 20th birthday one rainy night in Tokyo. Since none of the stories I had assembled focussed on the birthday of a young girl, I chose my character more or less consciously to supply that missing element.

As you will discover from reading this collection, the subject of birthdays yields surprisingly few happy stories, and several of them are quite dark. Even excluding "The Bath" as an extreme example, with its tale of a child who is run over and falls into a coma on his birthday, there are still a number of painful, heart-wrenching stories here: "Timothy's Birthday", in which a young man, feuding with his parents, can't (and won't) bring himself to go home on his birthday; "Dundun", in which a man, messed up on drugs, accidentally shoots his best friend; "The Birthday Cake", in which a lonely old woman stubbornly refuses to give a birthday cake to a young girl who will otherwise have none. Why should so many birthday stories be this gloomy? I suspect it is because the overwhelming majority of novelists are, by nature, incapable of taking the world at face value. If most people imagine candles on a cake and the singing of "Happy Birthday", conversely, a novelist who hears the word "birthday" is probably going to think, "Let me give them an *un*-happy birthday". That's my guess, at least. Take, for example, "The Emperor Who Had No Skin", in Lynda Sexson's "Turning", which at first glance appears to be an innocent fable. Why would three old ladies come to a boy's birthday party and tell the tale of an emperor with no skin? That alone can give anyone pause for thought and leave them with a strange, unsettled feeling.

By contrast we come away from Ethan Canin's story

with a real sense of relief. The central figure may be the same kind of crotchety old woman as in "The Birthday Cake", but, during her dealings with the crow that flies into her room and the kind-hearted lady from the animal shelter, her attitude softens somewhat. The elegant humour that pervades the story is a true delight. "The Moor" is another touching tale. A middle-aged man and an old woman meet unexpectedly one snowy night and recall their past love affair. The title is particularly stylish. A marvellous freshness disseminates through David Foster Wallace's "Forever Overhead" as it depicts a quiet summer day in the life of a boy on the verge of adulthood. The details, sensual descriptions of smell and light and the touch of the wind, are superb.

In dealing with the theme of giving a "lover for a night" to one's companion as a birthday gift, Andrea Lee's "The Birthday Present" and Paul Theroux's "A Game of Dice" are in a kind of gentle competition, though from opposite gender positions. Both stories leave the reader unsure whether to judge the ending as happy or unhappy. To tell you the truth, even I remain undecided whether it was necessary to go to quite such lengths for a birthday present. I don't know about you, but if someone gave me a gift like that (and, to date, no-one has), it would just stress me out.

I happened to find Claire Keegan's "Close to the Water's Edge" after the Japanese edition of this book had been published. Reading it left me with such a good feeling that I decided to add it to the English edition. Like Trevor, Keegan is an Irish writer. The two share what feels like a thoroughly natural commitment to storytelling, which may be something that springs from the Irish soil. In any case, I was glad to have discovered yet another outstanding work on the birthday theme.

"Ride" is a delightful story (with a touch of melancholy) by the young American writer Lewis Robinson. As I point out in the introduction to the story, Robinson's debut collection, *Officer Friendly*, contains another wonderful story with a birthday theme, and I had a hard time deciding which one to choose. Finally, the sad character of the father in "Ride" won me over.

Finally, as editor (and, in the one case, as author), I hope you find at least one story in the thirteen contained in this volume, whether happy or not, that gives you real pleasure and makes you want to spend part of your next birthday re-reading it. As long as this earth of ours continues to circle around the sun, your birthday will come around once a year and, whether or not it gets reported on the radio, for you it will be a special day.

Russell Banks
(Born in Massachusetts, 1940)

Banks is unquestionably one of the most powerful contemporary American writers, and I make a point of reading all his new work. His stories always move in a clear, straight line. Of course, he may not appeal to every reader: his heroes are invariably working-class white men with dark obsessions and anguished stories of self-destruction.

Banks' stories are not discussed as often as his forceful (sometimes, too forceful) novels, but one occasionally finds a piece as agreeable as "The Moor" in which the author has somewhat lowered the level of intensity. The story, which appeared in *The Angel on the Roof* (2000), is an unusually heartwarming piece for Banks, but the particular dark sense of pain that lingers after you have finished reading marks it as an unmistakable product of his world. It makes an excellent beginning for this anthology.

The Moor

BY RUSSELL BANKS

It's about 10:00 P.M., and I'm one of three, face it, middle-aged guys crossing South Main Street in light snow, headed for a quick drink at the Greek's. We've just finished a thirty-second-degree induction ceremony at the Masonic hall in the old Capitol Theater building and need a blow. I'm the tall figure in the middle, Warren Low, and I guess it's my story I'm telling, although you could say it was Gail Fortunata's story, since meeting her that night after half a lifetime is what got me started.

I'm wearing remnants of makeup from the ceremony, in which I portrayed an Arab prince – red lips, streaks of black on my face here and there, not quite washed off because of no cold cream at the Hall. The guys tease me about what a terrific nigger I make, that's the way they talk, and I try to deflect their teasing by ignoring it, because I'm not as prejudiced as they are, even though I'm pleased nonetheless. It's an acting job, the thirty-second, and not many guys are good at it. We are friends and businessmen, colleagues – I sell plumbing and heating supplies, my friend Sammy Gibson is in real estate, and the other, Rick Buckingham, is a Chevy dealer.

We enter the Greek's, a small restaurant and fern bar, pass through the dining room into the bar in back like regulars, because we are regulars and like making a point of it, greeting the Greek and his help. Small comforts. Sammy and Rick hit uselessly on one of the waitresses, the pretty little blond kid, and make a crack or two about the new gay waiter who's in the far corner by the kitchen door and can't hear them. Wise guys.

The Greek says to me, What's with the greasepaint? Theater group, I tell him. He's not a Mason, I think he's Orthodox Catholic or something, but he knows what we do. As we pass one table in particular, this elderly lady in the group looks me straight in the eyes, which gets my attention, because otherwise she's just some old lady. Then for a split second I think I know her, but decide not and keep going. She's a large, baggy, bright-eyed woman in her late seventies, possibly early eighties. Old.

Sammy, Rick, and I belly up to the bar, order drinks, the usuals, comment on the snow outside, and feel safe and contented in each other's company. We reflect on our wives and ex-wives and our grown kids, all elsewhere. We're out late and guilt-free.

I peek around the divider at her – thin, silver-blue hair, dewlaps at her throat, liver spots on her long flat cheeks. What the hell, an old lady. She's with family, some kind of celebration – two sons, they look like, in their forties, with their wives and a bored teenage girl, all five of them over-weight, dull, dutiful, in contrast to the old woman, who despite her age looks smart, aware, all dressed up in a maroon knit wool suit. Clearly an attractive woman once.

I drift from Sammy and Rick, ask the Greek, "Who's the old lady, what's the occasion?"

The Greek knows her sons' name, Italian – Fortunata, he thinks. "Doesn't register," I say. "No comprendo."

"The old lady's eightieth," says the Greek. "We should live so long, right? You know her?"

"No, I guess not." The waitresses and the gay waiter sing "Happy Birthday", making a scene, but the place is almost empty anyhow, from the snow, and everybody seems to like it, and the old lady smiles serenely.

I say to Sammy and Rick, "I think I know the old gal from someplace, but can't remember where."

"Customer," says Sammy, munching peanuts.

Rick says the same, "Customer," and they go on as before.

"Probably an old girlfriend," Sammy adds.

"Ha-ha," I say back.

A Celtics-Knicks game on TV has their attention, double overtime. Finally the Knicks win, and it's time to go home, guys. Snow's piling up. We pull on our coats, pay the bartender, and, as we leave, the old lady's party is also getting ready to go, and when I pass their table, she catches my sleeve, says my name. Says it with a question mark. "Warren? Warren Low?"

I say, "Yeah, hi," and smile, but still I don't remember her.

Then she says, "I'm Gail Fortunata. Warren, I knew you years ago," she says, and she smiles fondly. And then everything comes back, or almost everything. "Do you remember me?" she asks.

"Sure, sure I do, of course I do. Gail. How've you been? Jeeze, it's sure been a while."

She nods, still smiling. "What's that on your face? Makeup?"

"Yeah. Been doing a little theater. Didn't have any cold cream to get it all off," I say lamely.

She says, "I'm glad you're still acting." And then she introduces me to her family, like that, "This is my family."

"Howdy," I say, and start to introduce my friends Sammy and Rick, but they're already at the door.

Sammy says, "S'long, Warren, don't do anything I wouldn't do," and Rick gives a wave, and they're out.

"So, it's your birthday, Gail. Happy birthday."

She says, "Why, thank you." The others are all standing now, pulling on their coats, except for Gail, who still hasn't let go of my sleeve, which she tugs and then says to me, "Sit down a minute, Warren. I haven't seen you in what, thirty years. Imagine."

"Ma," the son says. "It's late. The snow."

I draw up a chair next to Gail, and, letting go of the dumb pretenses, I suddenly find myself struggling to see in her eyes the woman I knew for a few months when I was a kid, barely twenty-one, and she was almost fifty and married and these two fat guys were her skinny teenage sons. But I can't see through the old lady's face to the woman she was then. If that woman is gone, then so is the boy, this boy.

She looks up at one of her sons and says, "Dickie, you go without me. Warren will give me a ride, won't you, Warren?" she says, turning to me. "I'm staying at Dickie's house up on the Heights. That's not out of your way, is it?"

"Nope. I'm up on the Heights, too. Alton Woods. Just moved into a condo there."

Dickie says, "Fine," a little worried. He looks like he's used to losing arguments with his mother. They all give her a kiss on the cheek, wish her a happy birthday again, and file out into the snow. A plow scrapes past on the street. Otherwise, no traffic.

The Greek and his crew start cleaning up, while Gail and I talk a few minutes more. Although her eyes are wet and red-rimmed, she's not teary, she's smiling. It's as if there are translucent shells over her bright blue eyes. Even so, now when I look hard I can glimpse her the way she was, slipping around back there in the shadows. She had heavy, dark red hair, clear white skin smooth as porcelain, broad shoulders, and she was tall for a woman, almost as tall as I was, I remember exactly, from when she and her husband once took me along with them to a VFW party, and she and I danced while he played cards.

"You have turned into a handsome man, Warren," she says. Then she gives a little laugh. "Still a handsome man, I mean."

"Naw. Gone to seed. You're only young once, I guess."

"When we knew each other, Warren, I was the age you are now."

"Yeah. I guess that's so. Strange to think about, isn't it?"

"Are you divorced? You look like it."

"Yeah, divorced. Couple of years now. Kids, three girls, all grown up. I'm even a grandpa. It was not one of your happy marriages. Not by a long shot."

"I don't think I want to hear about all that."

"Okay. What do you want to hear about?"

"Let's have one drink and one short talk. For old times' sake. Then you may drive me to my son's home."

I say fine and ask the Greek, who's at the register tapping out, if it's too late for a nightcap. He shrugs why not, and Gail asks for a sherry and I order the usual, vodka and tonic. The Greek scoots back to the bar, pours the drinks himself because the bartender is wiping down the cooler, and returns and sets them down before us. "On the house," he says, and goes back to counting the night's take.

"It's odd, isn't it, that we never ran into each other before this," she says. "All these years. You came up here to Concord, and I stayed there in Portsmouth, even after the boys left. Frank's job was there."

"Yeah, well, I guess fifty miles is a long ways sometimes. How is Frank?" I ask, realizing as soon as I say it that he was at least ten years older than she.

"He died. Frank died in nineteen eighty-two."

"Oh, jeez. I'm sorry to hear that."

"I want to ask you something, Warren. I hope you won't mind if I speak personally with you."

"No. Shoot." I take a belt from my drink.

"I never dared to ask you then. It would have embarrassed you then, I thought, because you were so scared of what we were doing together, so unsure of yourself."

"Yeah, no kidding. I was what, twenty-one? And you were, well not scary, but let's say impressive. Married with kids, a sophisticated woman of the world, you seemed to me. And I was this apprentice plumber working on my first job away from home, a kid."

"You were more than that, Warren. That's why I took to you so easily. You were very sensitive. I thought someday you'd become a famous actor. I wanted to encourage you."

"You did." I laugh nervously because I don't know where this conversation is going and take another pull from my drink and say, "I've done lots of acting over the years, you know, all local stuff, some of it pretty serious. No big deal. But I kept it up. I don't do much nowadays, of course. But you did encourage me, Gail, you did, and I'm truly grateful for that."

She sips her sherry with pursed lips, like a bird. "Good," she says. "Warren, were you a virgin then, when you met me?"

"Oh, jeez. Well, that's quite a question, isn't it?" I laugh. "Is that what you've been wondering all these years? Were you the first woman I ever made love with? Wow. That's . . . Hey, Gail, I don't think anybody's ever asked me that before. And here we are, thirty years later." I'm smiling at her, but the air is rushing out of me.

"I just want to know, dear. You never said it one way or the other. We shared a big secret, but we never really talked about our own secrets. We talked about the theater, and we had our little love affair, and then you went on, and I stayed with Frank and grew old. Older."

"You weren't old."

"As old as you are now, Warren."

"Yes. But I'm not old."

"Well, were you?"

"What? A virgin?"

"You don't have to answer, if it embarrasses you."

I hold off a few seconds. The waitress and the new kid and the bartender have all left, and only the Greek is here, perched on a stool in the bar watching *Nightline*. I could tell her the truth, or I could lie, or I could beg off the question altogether. It's hard to know what's right. Finally, I say, "Yes, I was. I was a virgin when I met you. It was the first time for me," I tell her, and she sits back in her chair and looks me full in the face and smiles as if I've just given her the perfect birthday gift, the one no one else thought she wanted, the gift she never dared to ask for. It's a beautiful smile, grateful and proud and seems to go all the way back to the day we first met.

She reaches over and places her small, crackled hand on mine. She says, "I never knew for sure. But whenever I think back on those days and remember how we used to meet in your room, I always pretend that for you it was the first time. I even pretended it back then, when it was happening. It means something to me."

For a few moments neither of us speaks. Then I break the spell. "What do you say we shove off? They need to close this place up, and the snow's coming down hard." She agrees, and I help her slide into her coat. My car is parked only halfway down the block, but it's a slow walk to it, because the sidewalk is a little slippery and she's very careful.

When we're in the car and moving north on Main Street, we remain silent for a while, and finally I say to her,

"You know, Gail, there's something I've wondered all these years myself."

"Is there?"

"Yeah. But you don't have to tell me, if it embarrasses you."

"Warren, dear, you reach a certain age, nothing embarrasses you."

"Yeah, well. I guess that's true."

"What is it?"

"Okay, I wondered if, except for me, you stayed faithful to Frank. And before me."

No hesitation. She says, "Yes. I was faithful to Frank, before you and after. Except for my husband, you were the only man I loved."

I don't believe her, but I know why she has lied to me. This time it's my turn to smile and reach over and place my hand on hers.

The rest of the way we don't talk, except for her giving me directions to her son's house, which is a plain brick ranch on a curving side street by the old armory. The porch light is on, but the rest of the house is dark. "It's late," I say to her.

"So it is."

I get out and come around and help her from the car and then walk her up the path to the door. She gets her key from her purse and unlocks the door and turns around and looks up at me. She's not as tall as she used to be.

"I'm very happy that we saw each other tonight," she says. "We probably won't see each other again."

"Well, we can. If you want to."

23

"You're still a very sweet man, Warren. I'm glad of that. I wasn't wrong about you."

I don't know what to say. I want to kiss her, though, and I do, I lean down and put my arms around her and kiss her on the lips, very gently, then a little more, and she kisses me back, with just enough pressure against me to let me know that she is remembering everything, too. We hold each other like that for a long time.

Then I step away, and she turns, opens the door, and takes one last look back at me. She smiles. "You've still got makeup on," she says. "What's the play? I forgot to ask."

"Oh," I say, thinking fast, because I'm remembering that she's Catholic and probably doesn't think much of the Masons. "*Othello*," I say.

"That's nice, and you're the Moor?"

"Yes."

Still smiling, she gives me a slow pushing wave with her hand, as if dismissing me, and goes inside. When the door has closed behind her, I want to stand there alone on the steps all night with the snow falling around my head in clouds and watch it fill our tracks on the path. But it actually is late, and I have to work tomorrow, so I leave.

Driving home, it's all I can do to keep from crying. Time's come, time's gone, time's never returning, I say to myself. What's here in front of me is all I've got, I decide, and as I drive my car through the blowing snow it doesn't seem like much, except for the kindness that I've just exchanged with an old lady, so I concentrate on that.

Denis Johnson
(Born in Munich, 1949)

Johnson is an outstanding writer of tremendous power, but his work is not for everybody. He can be uneven, too, like a great pitcher who occasionally lets the ball decide where it's going. Johnson says that he began writing under the influence of Jimi Hendrix's guitar solos, and you kind of understand what he means. His collection *Jesus' Son*, though, is a thoroughgoing masterpiece. Every one of its stories can be recommended to readers who enjoy contemporary fiction with an edge.

"Dundun" appeared in that collection. It is a short piece, but its blunt narrative voice and bone-dry violence leave a strange weight in the heart. Where do people come from, where are they going and is there such a thing as salvation? Whatever the answers to these questions may be, for Dundun there was only one way he could have spent this birthday.

Dundun

BY DENIS JOHNSON

I went out to the farmhouse where Dundun lived to get some pharmaceutical opium from him, but I was out of luck.

He greeted me as he was coming out into the front yard to go to the pump, wearing new cowboy boots and a leather vest, with his flannel shirt hanging out over his jeans. He was chewing on a piece of gum.

"McInnes isn't feeling too good today. I just shot him."

"You mean killed him?"

"I didn't mean to."

"Is he really dead?"

"No. He's sitting down."

"But he's alive."

"Oh, sure, he's alive. He's sitting down now in the back room."

Dundun went on over to the pump and started working the handle.

I went around the house and in through the back. The room just through the back door smelled of dogs and babies. Beatle stood in the opposite doorway. She watched me come in. Leaning against the wall was Blue, smoking a cigarette and scratching her chin thoughtfully. Jack Hotel was over at an old desk, setting fire to a pipe the bowl of which was wrapped in tinfoil.

When they saw it was only me, the three of them resumed looking at McInnes, who sat on the couch all alone, with his left hand resting gently on his belly.

"Dundun shot him?" I asked.

"Somebody shot somebody," Hotel said.

Dundun came in behind me carrying some water in a china cup and a bottle of beer and said to McInnes: "Here."

"*I* don't want that," McInnes said.

"Okay. Well, here, then." Dundun offered him the rest of his beer.

"No thanks."

I was worried. "Aren't you taking him to the hospital or anything?"

"Good idea," Beatle said sarcastically.

"We started to," Hotel explained, "but we ran into the corner of the shed out there."

I looked out the side window. This was Tim Bishop's farm. Tim Bishop's Plymouth, I saw, which was a very nice old grey-and-red sedan, had sideswiped the shed and replaced one of the corner posts, so that the post lay on the ground and the car now held up the shed's roof.

"The front windshield is in millions of bits," Hotel said.

"How'd you end up way over there?"

"Everything was completely out of hand," Hotel said.

"Where's Tim, anyway?"

"He's not here," Beatle said.

Hotel passed me the pipe. It was hashish, but it was pretty well burned up already.

"How you doing?" Dundun asked McInnes.

"I can feel it right here. It's just stuck in the muscle."

Dundun said, "It's not bad. The cap didn't explode right, I think."

"It misfired."

"It misfired a little bit, yeah."

Hotel asked me, "Would you take him to the hospital in your car?"

"Okay," I said.

"I'm coming, too," Dundun said.

"Have you got any of the opium left?" I asked him.

"No," he said. "That was a birthday present. I used it all up."

"When's your birthday?" I asked him.

"Today."

"You shouldn't have used it all up before your birthday, then," I told him angrily.

But I was happy about this chance to be of use. I wanted to be the one who saw it through and got McInnes to the doctor without a wreck. People would talk about it, and I hoped I would be liked.

In the car were Dundun, McInnes, and myself.

This was Dundun's twenty-first birthday. I'd met him in the Johnson County facility during the only few days I'd ever spent in jail, around the time of my eighteenth Thanksgiving. I was the older of us by a month of two. As for McInnes, he'd been around forever, and in fact, I, myself, was married to one of his old girlfriends.

We took off as fast as I could go without bouncing the shooting victim around too heavily.

Dundun said, "What about the brakes? You get them working?"

"The emergency brake does. That's enough."

"What about the radio?" Dundun punched the button, and the radio came on making an emission like a meat grinder.

He turned it off and then on, and now it burbled like a machine that polishes stones all night.

"How about you?" I asked McInnes. "Are you comfortable?"

"What do you think?" McInnes said.

It was a long straight road through dry fields as far as a person could see. You'd think the sky didn't have any air in it, and the earth was made of paper. Rather than moving, we were just getting smaller and smaller.

What can be said about those fields? There were blackbirds circling above their own shadows, and beneath them the cows stood around smelling one another's butts. Dundun spat his gum out the window while digging in his shirt pocket for his Winstons. He lit a Winston with a match. That was all there was to say.

"We'll never get off this road," I said.

"What a lousy birthday," Dundun said.

McInnes was white and sick, holding himself tenderly. I'd seen him like that once or twice even when he hadn't been shot. He had a bad case of hepatitis that often gave him a lot of pain.

"Do you promise not to tell them anything?" Dundun was talking to McInnes.

"I don't think he hears you," I said.

"Tell them it was an accident, okay?"

McInnes said nothing for a long moment. Finally he said, "Okay."

"Promise?" Dundun said.

But McInnes said nothing. Because he was dead.

Dundun looked at me with tears in his eyes. "What do you say?"

"What do you mean, what do I say? Do you think I'm here because I know all about this stuff?"

"He's dead."

"All *right*. I *know* he's dead."

"Throw him out of the car."

"Damn right throw him out of the car," I said. "I'm not taking him anywhere now."

For a moment I fell asleep, right while I was driving. I had a dream in which I was trying to tell someone something and they kept interrupting, a dream about frustration.

"I'm glad he's dead," I told Dundun. "He's the one who started everybody calling me Fuckhead."

Dundun said, "Don't let it get you down."

We whizzed along down through the skeleton remnants of Iowa.

"I wouldn't mind working as a hit man," Dundun said.

Glaciers had crushed this region in the time before history. There'd been a drought for years, and a bronze fog of dust stood over the plains. The soybean crop was dead again, and the failed, wilted cornstalks were laid out on the ground like rows of underthings. Most of the farmers didn't even plant anymore. All the false visions had been erased. It felt like the moment before the Savior comes. And the Savior did come, but we had to wait a long time.

Dundun tortured Jack Hotel at the lake outside of Denver. He did this to get information about a stolen item, a stereo belonging to Dundun's girlfriend, or perhaps to his sister. Later, Dundun beat a man almost to death with a tire iron right on the street in Austin, Texas, for which he'll also someday have to answer, but now he is, I think, in the state prison in Colorado.

Will you believe me when I tell you there was kindness in his heart? His left hand didn't know what his right hand was doing. It was only that certain important connections had been burned through. If I opened up your head and ran a hot soldering iron around in your brain, I might turn you into someone like that.

William Trevor
(Born in Ireland, 1928)

Ever since his debut in the late 1950s, William Trevor has published many novels and stories that have won high praise throughout the world. *After Rain*, the collection containing the story "Timothy's Birthday", appeared in 1990. Trevor's fictive world is often an exact counterpart of Ireland's overcast skies: dark, leaden, doomed. His people trudge on in silence bearing the burdens they have been given, never to be relieved of their crushing weight. It has been written of Trevor that, though his work portrays despair, it never leaves his readers despairing.

Trevor's work is notable for its precision of style and complexity of vision: his descriptions are fresh and clear without an ounce of excess weight, and the detailed, unwavering observation of his characters can be as sharp as a knife yet still contain a strange tenderness. "Timothy's Birthday" is no exception. Anyone who has been to Ireland will recognise, too, the faithful depiction of the Irish landscape.

Timothy's Birthday

BY WILLIAM TREVOR

They made the usual preparations. Charlotte bought a small leg of lamb, picked purple broccoli and sprigs of mint. All were Timothy's favourites, purchased every year for April 23rd, which this year was a Thursday. Odo ensured that the gin had not gone too low: a gin and tonic, and then another one, was what Timothy liked. Odo did not object to that, did not in fact object to obtaining the gin specially, since it was not otherwise drunk in the house.

They were a couple in their sixties who had scarcely parted from each other in the forty-two years of their marriage. Odo was tall, thin as a straw, his bony features receding into a freckled dome on which little hair remained. Charlotte was small and still pretty, her grey hair drawn back and tidy, her eyes an arresting shade of blue. Timothy was their only child.

Deciding on a fire, Odo chopped up an old seed-box for kindling and filled a basket with logs and turf. The rocks were cawing and chattering in the high trees, their nests already in place – more of them this year, Odo noticed, than last. The cobbles of the yard were still damp from a shower. Grass, occasionally ragwort or a dock, greened them in patches. Later perhaps, when Timothy had gone, he'd go over them with weed-killer, as he did every year in April. The outhouses that bounded the yard required attention also, their wooden doors rotted away at the bottom, the whitewash of their stucco gone grey, brambles growing through their windows. Odo resolved that this year he would rectify matters, but knew, even as the thought occurred, that he would not.

"Cold?" Charlotte asked him as he passed through the kitchen, and he said yes, a little chilly outside. The kitchen was never cold because of the range. A long time ago they had been going to replace it with a secondhand Aga Charlotte had heard about, but when it came to the point Odo hadn't wanted to and anyway there hadn't been the funds.

In the drawing-room Odo set the fire, crumpling up the pages of old account books because no newspaper was delivered to the house and one was rarely bought: they had the wireless and the television, which kept them up with things. The account books were of no use to anyone, belonging entirely to the past, to the time of Odo's grand-father and generations earlier. Kept for the purpose in a wall-cupboard by the fireplace, their dry pages never failed to burn well. *Slating: £2.15s.*, Odo read as he arranged the kindling over the slanted calligraphy. He struck a match and stacked on logs and turf. Rain spattered against the long-paned windows; a sudden gust of wind tumbled something over in the garden.

Charlotte pressed rosemary into the slits she'd incised in the lamb. She worked swiftly, from long experience knowing just what she was doing. She washed the grease from her fingertips under a running tap and set aside what remained of the rosemary, even though it was unlikely that she would have a use for it: she hated throwing things away.

The oven was slow; although it was still early, the meat would have to go in within half an hour, and potatoes to roast – another Timothy favourite – at eleven. The trifle, gooey with custard and raspberry jam and jelly – a nursery pudding – Charlotte had made the night before. When Timothy came he chopped the mint for the mint sauce, one of the first of his childhood tasks. He'd been a plump little boy then.

*

"I can't go," Timothy said in the flat that had recently been left to him by Mr Kinnally.

Eddie didn't respond. He turned the pages of the *Irish Times*, wishing it were something livelier, the *Star* or the *Express*. With little interest he noticed that schools' entrance tests were to be abolished and that there was to be a canine clean-up, whatever that was, in Limerick.

"I'll drive you down," he offered then. His own plans were being shattered by this change of heart on the part of Timothy, but he kept the annoyance out of his voice. He had intended to gather his belongings together and leave as soon as he had the house to himself: a bus out of the N4, the long hitch-hike, then start all over again. "No problem to drive you down," he said. "No problem."

The suggestion wasn't worth a reply, Timothy considered. It wasn't even worth acknowledgement. No longer plump at thirty-three, Timothy wore his smooth fair hair in a ponytail. When he smiled, a dimple appeared in his left cheek, a characteristic he cultivated. He was dressed, this morning, as he often was, in flannel trousers and a navy-blue blazer, with a plain blue tie in the buttoned-down collar of his plain blue shirt.

"I'd get out before we got there," Eddie offered. "I'd go for a walk while you was inside."

"What I'm saying is I can't face it."

There was another silence then, during which Eddie sighed without making a sound. He knew about the birthday tradition because as the day approached there had been a lot of talk about it. The house called Coolattin had been described to him: four miles from the village of Baltinglass, a short avenue from which the entrance gates had been removed, a faded green hall-door, the high grass in the garden, the abandoned conservatory. And Timothy's people – as Timothy always called them – had been as graphically presented: Charlotte's smile and Odo's solemnity, their fondness for one another evident in how they spoke and acted, their fondness for Coolattin. Charlotte cut what remained of Odo's hair, and Timothy said you could tell. And you could tell, even when they were not in their own surroundings, that they weren't well-to-do: all they wore was old. Hearing it described, Eddie had visualized in the drawing-room the bagatelle table between the windows and Odo's ancestor in oils over the fireplace, the buttoned green sofa, the rugs that someone had once brought back from India or Egypt. Such shreds of grace and vigour from a family's past took similar form in the dining-room that was these days used only once a year, on April 23rd, and in the hall and on the staircase wall, where further portraits hung. Except for the one occupied by Odo and Charlotte, the bedrooms were musty, with patches of grey damp on the ceilings, and plaster fallen away. Timothy's, in which he had not slept for fifteen years, was as he'd left it, but in one corner the wallpaper had billowed out and now was curling away from the surface. The kitchen, where the television and the wireless were, where Odo and Charlotte ate all their meals except for lunch on Timothy's birthday, was easily large enough for this general purpose: a dresser crowded with crockery and a lifetime's odds and ends, a long scrubbed table on the flagged floor, with upright kitchen chairs around it. As well, there were the two armchairs Odo had brought in from the drawing-room, a washing-machine Timothy had given his mother, wooden draining-boards on either side of the sink, ham hooks in the panelled ceiling, and a row of bells on springs above the door to the scullery. A cheerful place, that kitchen, Eddie estimated, but Timothy said it was part and parcel, whatever he meant by that.

"Would you go, Eddie? Would you go down and explain, say I'm feeling unwell?"

Eddie hesitated. Then he said:

"Did Mr Kinnally ever go down there?"

"No, of course he didn't. It's not the same."

Eddie walked away when he heard that reply. Mr Kinnally had been far too grand to act as a messenger in that way. Mr Kinnally had given Timothy birthday presents: the chain he wore on his wrist, shoes and pullovers. "Now, I don't want you spending your money on me," Timothy had said a day or two ago. Eddie, who hadn't been intending to, didn't even buy a card.

In the kitchen he made coffee, real coffee from Bewley's, measured into the percolator, as Timothy had shown him. Instant gave you cancer, Timothy maintained. Eddie was a burly youth of nineteen, with curly black hair to which he daily applied gel. His eyes, set on a slant, gave him a furtive air, accurately reflecting his nature, which was a watchful one, the main chance being never far out of his sights. When he got away from the flat in Mountjoy Street he intended to go steady for a bit, maybe settle down with some decent girl, maybe have a kid. Being in the flat had suited him for the five months he'd been here, even if – privately – he didn't much care for certain aspects of the arrangement. Once, briefly, Eddie had been apprenticed to a plumber, but he hadn't much cared for that either.

He arranged cups and saucers on a tray and carried them to the sitting-room, with the coffee and milk, and a plate of croissants. Timothy had put a CD on, the kind of music Eddie didn't care for but never said so, sonorous and grandiose. The hi-fi was Bang and Olufsen, the property of Mr Kinnally in his lifetime, as everything in the flat had been.

"Why not?" Timothy asked, using the telecommander on the arm of his chair to turn the volume down. "Why not, Eddie?"

"I couldn't do a thing like that. I'll drive you—"

"I'm not going down."

Timothy reduced the volume further. As he took the cup of coffee Eddie offered him, his two long eye-teeth glistened the way they sometimes did, and the dimple formed in his cheek.

"All I'm asking you to do is pass a message on. I'd take it as a favour."

"The phone—"

"There's no phone in that place. Just say I couldn't make it due to not feeling much today."

Timothy broke in half a croissant that had specks of bacon in it, the kind he liked, that Eddie bought in Fitz's. A special favour, he softly repeated, and Eddie sensed more pressure in the words. Timothy paid, Timothy called the tune. Well, two can play at that game, Eddie said to himself, and calculated his gains over the past five months.

*

The faded green hall-door, green also on the inside, was sealed up because of draughts. You entered the house at the back, crossing the cobbled yard to the door that led to the scullery.

"He's here," Charlotte called out when there was the sound of a car, and a few minutes later, as Odo arrived in the kitchen from the hall, there were footsteps in the scullery passage and then a hesitant knock on the kitchen door. Since Timothy never knocked, both thought this odd, and odder still when a youth they did not know appeared.

"Oh," Charlotte said.

"He's off colour," the youth said. "A bit naff today. He asked me would I come down and tell you." The youth paused, and added then: "On account you don't have no phone."

Colour crept into Charlotte's face, her cheeks becoming pink. Illness worried her.

"Thank you for letting us know," Odo said stiffly, the dismissive note in his tone willing this youth to go away again.

"It's nothing much, is it?" Charlotte asked, and the youth said seedy, all morning in the toilet, the kind of thing you wouldn't trust yourself with on a car journey. His name was Eddie, he explained, a friend of Timothy's. Or more, he added, a servant really, depending how you looked at it.

Odo tried not to think about this youth. He didn't want Charlotte to think about him, just as for so long he hadn't wanted her to think about Mr Kinnally. "Mr Kinnally died," Timothy said on this day last year, standing not far from where the youth was standing now, his second gin and tonic on the go. "He left me everything, the flat, the Rover, the lot." Odo had experienced relief that this elderly man was no longer alive, but had been unable to prevent himself from considering the inheritance ill-gotten. The flat in Mountjoy Street, well placed in Dublin, had had its Georgian plasterwork meticulously restored, for Mr Kinnally had been that kind of person. They'd heard about the flat, its contents too, just as Eddie had heard about Coolattin. Timothy enjoyed describing things.

"His tummy played up a bit once," Charlotte was

saying with a mother's recall. "We had a scare. We thought appendicitis. But it wasn't in the end."

"He'll rest himself, he'll be all right." The youth was mumbling, not meeting the eye of either of them. Shifty, Odo considered, and dirty-looking. The shoes he wore, once white, the kind of sports shoes you saw about these days, were filthy now. His black trousers hung shapelessly; his neck was bare, no sign of shirt beneath the red sweater that had some kind of animal depicted on it.

"Thank you," Odo said again.

"A drink?" Charlotte offered. "Cup of coffee? Tea?"

Odo had known that would come. No matter what the circumstances, Charlotte could never help being hospitable. She hated being thought otherwise.

"Well . . ." the youth began, and Charlotte said:

"Sit down for a minute." Then she changed her mind and suggested the drawing-room because it was a pity to waste the fire.

Odo didn't feel angry. He rarely did with Charlotte. "I'm afraid we haven't any beer," he said as they passed through the hall, both coffee and tea having been rejected on the grounds that they would be troublesome to provide, although Charlotte had denied that. In the drawing-room what there was was the sherry that stood near the bagatelle, never touched by either of them, and Timothy's Cork gin, and two bottles of tonic.

"I'd fancy a drop of Cork," the youth said. "If that's OK."

Would Timothy come down another day? Charlotte wanted to know. Had he said anything about that? It was the first time his birthday had been missed. It was the one occasion they spent together, she explained.

"Cheers!" the youth exclaimed, not answering the questions, appearing to Odo to be simulating denseness. "Great," he complimented when he'd sipped the gin.

"Poor Timothy!" Charlotte settled into the chair she always occupied in the drawing-room, to the left of the fire. The light from the long-paned windows fell on her neat grey hair and the side of her face. One of them would die first, Odo had thought again in the night, as he often did now. He wanted it to be her; he wanted to be the one to suffer the loneliness and the distress. It would be the same for either of them, and he wanted it to be him who had to bear the painful burden.

*

Sitting forward, on the edge of the sofa, Eddie felt better when the gin began to glow.

"Refreshing," he said. "A drop of Cork."

The day Mr Kinnally died there were a number of them in the flat. Timothy put the word out and they came that night, with Mr Kinnally still stretched out on his bed. In those days Eddie used to come in the mornings to do the washing-up, after Mr Kinnally had taken a fancy to him in O'Connell Street. An hour or so in the mornings, last night's dishes, paid by the hour; nothing of the other, he didn't even know about it then. On the day of the death Timothy shaved the dead face himself and got Mr Kinnally into his tweeds. He sprayed a little Krizia Uomo, and changed the slippers for lace-ups. He made him as he had been, except of course for the closed eyes, you couldn't do anything about that. "Come back in the evening, could you?" he had requested Eddie, the first time there'd been such a summons. "There'll be a few here." There were more than a few, paying their respects in the bedroom, and afterwards in the sitting-room Timothy put on the music and they just sat there. From the scraps of conversation that were exchanged Eddie learned that Timothy had inherited, that Timothy was in the dead man's shoes, the new Mr Kinnally. "You'd never think of moving in, Eddie?" Timothy suggested a while later, and afterwards Eddie guessed that that was how Timothy himself had been invited to Mountjoy Street, when he was working in the newsagent's in Ballsbridge, on his uppers as he used to say.

"As a matter of fact," Eddie said in the drawing-room, "I never touch a beer."

Timothy's father – so thin and bony in Eddie's view that when he sat down you'd imagine it would cause him pain – gave a nod that was hardly a nod at all. And the mother said she couldn't drink beer in any shape or form. Neither of them was drinking now.

"Nothing in the gassy line suits me," Eddie confided. It wasn't easy to know what to say. Timothy had said they'd ask him to stop for a bite of grub when they realized he'd come down specially; before he knew where he was they'd have turned him into the birthday boy. Odo his father's name was, Timothy had passed on, extraordinary really.

"Nice home you got here," Eddie said. "Nice place."

A kind of curiosity had brought him to the house. Once Timothy had handed him the keys of the Rover, he could as easily have driven straight to Galway, which was the city he had decided to make for, having heard a few times that it was lively. But instead he'd driven as directed, to Baltinglass, and then by minor roads to Coolattin. He'd head for Galway later: the N80 to Portlaoise was what the map in the car indicated, then on to Mountmellick and Tullamore, then Athlone. Eddie didn't know any of those towns. Dublin was his place.

"Excuse me," he said, addressing Timothy's father, lowering his voice. "D'you have a toilet?"

*

Charlotte had years ago accepted her son's way of life. She had never fussed about it, and saw no reason to. Yet she sympathized with Odo, and was a little infected by the disappointment he felt. "This is how Timothy wishes to live," she used, once, gently to argue, but Odo would look away, saying he didn't understand it, saying – to Timothy, too – that he didn't want to know. Odo was like that; nothing was going to change him. Coolattin had defeated him, and he had always hoped, during Timothy's childhood, that Timothy would somehow make a go of it where he himself had failed. In those days they had taken in overnight guests, but more recently too much went wrong in the house, and the upkeep was too burdensome, to allow them to continue without financial loss. Timothy, as a child, had been both imaginative and practical: Odo had seen a time in the future when there would be a family at Coolattin again, when in some clever way both house and gardens would be restored. Timothy had even talked about it, describing it, as he liked to: a flowery hotel, the kitchen filled with modern utensils and machines, the bedrooms fresh with paint, new wallpapers and fabrics. Odo could recall a time in his own childhood when visitors came and went, not paying for their sojourn, of course, but visitors who paid would at least be something.

"You'll have to ask him if he wants to stay to lunch," Charlotte said when Timothy's friend had been shown where the downstairs lavatory was.

"Yes, I know."

*

"I'd fix that toilet for you," Eddie offered, explaining that the flow to the bowl was poor. Nothing complicated, corrosion in the pipe. He explained that he'd started out as a plumber once, which was why he knew a thing or two. "No sweat," he said.

When lunch was mentioned he said he wouldn't want to trouble anyone, but they said no trouble. He picked up a knife from the drinks table and set off with his gin and tonic to the downstairs lavatory to effect the repair.

"It's very kind of you, Eddie." Timothy's mother thanked him and he said honestly, no sweat.

When he returned to the drawing-room, having poked about in the cistern with the knife, the room was empty. Rain was beating against the windows. The fire had burnt low. He poured another dollop of gin into his glass, not bothering with the tonic since that would have meant opening the second bottle. Then the old fellow appeared out of nowhere with a basket of logs, causing Eddie to jump.

"I done it best I could," Eddie said, wondering if he'd been seen with the bottle actually in his hand and thinking he probably had. "It's better than it was anyway."

"Yes," Timothy's father said, putting a couple of the logs on to the fire and a piece of turf at the back. "Thanks very much."

"Shocking rain," Eddie said.

Yes, it was heavy now, the answer came, and nothing more was said until they moved into the dining-room. "You sit there, Eddie," Timothy's mother directed, and he sat as she indicated, between the two of them. A plate was passed to him with slices of meat on it, then vegetable dishes with potatoes and broccoli in them.

"It was a Thursday, too, the day Timothy was born," Timothy's mother said. "In the newspaper they brought me it said something about a royal audience with the Pope."

1959, Eddie calculated, fourteen years before he saw the light of day himself. He thought of mentioning that, but decided they wouldn't want to know. The drop of Cork had settled in nicely, the only pity was they hadn't brought the bottle in to the table.

"Nice bit of meat," he said instead, and she said it was Timothy's favourite, always had been. The old fellow was silent again. The old fellow hadn't believed him when he'd said Timothy was off colour. The old fellow knew exactly what was going on, you could tell that straight away.

"Pardon me a sec." Eddie rose, promoted by the fact

that he knew where both of them were. In the drawing-room he poured himself more gin, and grimaced as he swallowed it. He poured a smaller measure and didn't, this time, gulp it. In the hall he picked up a little ornament that might be silver: two entwined fish he had noticed earlier. In the lavatory he didn't close the door in the hope that they would hear the flush and assume he'd been there all the time.

"Great," he said in the dining-room as he sat down again.

The mother asked about his family. He mentioned Tallaght, no reason not to since it was what she was after. He referred to the tinker encampment, and said it was a bloody disgrace, tinkers allowed like that. "Pardon my French," he apologized when the swearword slipped out.

"More, Eddie?" she was saying, glancing at the old fellow since it was he who was in charge of cutting the meat.

"Yeah, great." He took his knife and fork off his plate, and after it was handed back to him there was a bit of a silence so he added:

"A new valve would be your only answer in the toilet department. No problem with your pressure."

"We must get it done," she said.

It was then – when another silence gathered and continued for a couple of minutes – that Eddie knew the mother had guessed also: suddenly it came into her face that Timothy was as fit as a fiddle. Eddie saw her glance once across the table, but the old fellow was intent on his food. On other birthday occasions Timothy would have talked about Mr Kinnally, about his "circle", which was how the friends who came to the flat were always described. Blearily, through a fog of Cork gin, Eddie knew all that, even heard the echo of Timothy's rather high-pitched voice at this same table. But talk about Mr Kinnally had never been enough.

"'Course it could go on the way it is for years," Eddie said, the silence having now become dense. "As long as there's a drop coming through at all you're in business with a toilet cistern."

He continued about the faulty valve, stumbling over some of the words, his speech thickened by the gin. From time to time the old man nodded, but no sign came from the mother. Her features were bleak now, quite unlike they'd been a moment ago, when she'd kept the conversation going. The two had met when she walked up the avenue of Coolattin one day, looking for petrol for her car: Timothy had reported that too. The car was broken down a mile away; she came to the first house there was, which happened to be Coolattin. They walked back to the car together and they fell in love. A Morris 8, Timothy said; 1950 it was. "A lifetime's celebration of love," he'd said that morning, in the toneless voice he sometimes adopted. "That's what you'll find down there."

It wouldn't have been enough, either, to have had Kinnally here in person. Kinnally they could have taken; Kinnally would have oozed about the place, remarking on the furniture and the pictures on the walls. Judicious, as he would have said himself, a favourite word. Kinnally could be judicious. Rough trade was different.

"There's trifle," Eddie heard the old woman say before she rose to get it.

*

The rain came in, heavier now, from the west. A signpost indicated Athlone ahead, and Eddie remembered being informed in a classroom that this town was more or less the centre of Ireland. He drove slowly. If for any reason a police car signalled him to stop he would be found to have more than the permitted quantity of alcohol in his bloodstream; if for any reason his clothing was searched he would be found to be in possession of stolen property; if he was questioned about the car he was driving he would not be believed when he said it had been earlier lent to him for a purpose.

The Rover's windscreen wipers softly swayed, the glass of the windscreen perfectly clear in their wake. Then a lorry went by, and threw up surface water from the road. On the radio Chris de Burgh sang.

The sooner he disposed of the bit of silver the better, Athlone maybe. In Galway he would dump the car in a car park somewhere. The single effect remaining after his intake of gin was the thirst he experienced, as dry as paper his mouth was.

He turned Chris de Burgh off, not trying another channel. It was one thing to scarper off, as Timothy had from that house: he'd scarpered himself from Tallaght. To turn the knife was different. Fifteen years later to make your point with rough trade and transparent lies, to lash out venomously: how had they cocked him up, how had they hurt him, to deserve it? All the time when there had been that silence they had gone on eating, as if leaving the food on their plates would be too dramatic a gesture. The old man nodded once or twice about the valve, but she had given no sign that she even heard. Very slightly, as he drove, Eddie's head began to ache.

"Pot of tea," he ordered in Athlone, and said no, nothing else when the woman waited. The birthday presents had remained on the sideboard, not given to him to deliver, as Timothy had said they probably would be. The two figures stood, hardly moving, at the back door while he hurried across the puddles in the cobbled yard to the car. When he looked back they were no longer there.

"Great," Eddie said when the woman brought the tea, in a metal pot, cup and saucer and a teaspoon. Milk and sugar were already on the pink patterned oilcoth that covered the table top. "Thanks," Eddie said, and when he had finished and had paid he walked through the rain, his headache clearing in the chilly air. In the first jeweller's shop the man said he didn't buy stuff. In the second Eddie was questioned so he said he came from Fardrum, a village he'd driven through. His mother had given him the thing to sell, he explained, the reason being she was sick in bed and needed a dose of medicine. But the jeweller frowned, and the trinket was handed back to him without a further exchange. In a shop that had ornaments and old books in the window Eddie was offered a pound and said he thought the entwined fish were worth more. "One fifty," came the offer then, and he accepted it.

It didn't cease to rain. As he drove on through it, Eddie

felt better because he'd sold the fish. He felt like stopping in Ballinasloe for another pot of tea but changed his mind. In Galway he dropped the car off in the first car park he came to.

*

Together they cleared away the dishes. Odo found that the gin in the drawing-room had been mostly drunk. Charlotte washed up at the sink. Then Odo discovered that the little ornament was gone from the hall and slowly went to break this news, the first communication between them since their visitor had left.

"These things happen," Charlotte said, after another silence.

*

The rain was easing when Eddie emerged from a public house in Galway, having been slaking his thirst with 7-Up and watching *Glenroe*. As he walked into the city, it dribbled away to nothing. Watery sunshine slipped through the unsettled clouds, brightening the façades in Eyre Square. He sat on a damp seat there, wondering about picking up a girl, but none passed by so he moved away. He didn't want to think. He wasn't meant to understand, being only what he was. Being able to read Timothy like a book was just a way of putting it, talking big when nobody could hear.

Yet the day still nagged, its images stumbling about, persisting in Eddie's bewilderment. Timothy smiled when he said all he was asking was that a message should be passed on. Eddie's own hand closed over the silver fish. In the dining-room the life drained out of her eyes. Rain splashed the puddles in the cobbled yard and they stood, not moving, in the doorway.

On the quays the breeze from the Atlantic dried the pale stone of the houses and cooled the skin of Eddie's face, freshening it also. People had come out to stroll, an old man with a smooth-haired terrier, a couple speaking a foreign language. Seagulls screeched, swooping and bickering in the air. It had been the natural thing to lift the ornament in the hall since it was there and no one was around: in fairness you could call it payment for scraping the rust off the ballcock valve, easily ten quid that would have cost them. "A lifetime's celebration," Timothy said again.

*

"It has actually cleared up," Odo said at the window, and Charlotte rose from the armchair by the fire and stood there with him, looking out at the drenched garden. They walked in it together when the last drops had fallen.

"Fairly battered the delphiniums," Odo said.

"Hasn't it just."

She smiled a little. You had to accept what there was; no point in brooding. They had been hurt, as was intended, punished because one of them continued to be disappointed and repelled. There never is fairness when vengeance is evoked: that had occurred to Charlotte when she was washing up the lunchtime dishes, and to Odo when he tidied the dining-room. "I'm sorry," he had said, returning to the kitchen with forks and spoons that had not been used. Not turning round, Charlotte had shaken her head.

They were not bewildered, as their birthday visitor was: they easily understood. Their own way of life was so much debris all around them, but since they were no longer in their prime that hardly mattered. Once it would have, Odo reflected now; Charlotte had known that years ago. Their love of each other had survived the vicissitudes and the struggle there had been; not even the bleakness of the day that had passed could affect it.

They didn't mention their son as they made their rounds of the garden that was now too much for them and was derelict in places. They didn't mention the jealousy their love of each other had bred in him, that had flourished into deviousness and cruelty. The pain the day had brought would not easily pass, both were aware of that. And yet it had to be, since it was part of what there was.

Daniel Lyons
(Born in Massachusetts, 1960)

Daniel Lyons lives in Charlestown, Massachusetts. A busy freelance journalist, Lyons also writes fiction and has published the short story collection, *The Last Good Man* (1993), from which "The Birthday Cake" is taken, and the novel *Dog Days* (1998). His story "Greyhound" won the Playboy College Fiction Award. One review of *The Last Good Man* said, "Despite the darkness he visits upon his characters, Lyons' stories leave the reader with an abiding sense of redemption, and a belief in the power of the human spirit to survive and to aspire to be good" (*Boston Book Review*).

Like Ethan Canin's "Angel of Mercy, Angel of Wrath", "The Birthday Cake" looks at a cross-grained old woman living a lonely life in the city, but the feel of these two birthday stories is very different. I hope you will compare them as you read.

The Birthday Cake

BY DANIEL LYONS

The air was cold and the daylight was draining from the sky. The street smelled of rotten fruit left in the carts and although this was a sour smell it was not altogether unpleasant. Lucia was accustomed to this odor, and because it reminded her of the feast days when she was a girl she enjoyed it, the way she imagined people on farms enjoyed the smell of manure.

It was past six and the shops on Newbury Street were closed, but she knew that Lorenzo would stay open for her. She did not hurry: she was an old woman, and age had spoiled her legs. They were thick now, and water heavy, and when she walked her hips grew sore from the effort of moving them.

She stopped by a bench, wanting to sit but knowing that to stoop and then to rise would be more difficult than simply to lean against the backrest. She waited for her breathing to slow, then walked the last block to the bakery. Lorenzo would be there. He would wait. Hadn't she come to the bakery every Saturday since the war? And hadn't she bought the same white cake with chocolate frosting, Nico's favorite?

"Buona sera, Signora Ronsavelli," he said as the chime

clanged and the heavy glass door closed behind her. "You had me concerned."

Lorenzo Napoli was too young to be so worried all the time. She wondered about him. She did not trust him the way she had trusted his father.

Standing before the pastry case was Maria Mendez, the little Puerto Rican girl who worked at the laundry. "Este es la señora," Lorenzo said to her. They were everywhere now, these Puerto Ricans, all over the neighborhood with their loud cars and shouting children and men drinking beer on the sidewalk. Now the rents were increasing and the real estate people wanted the Italians to move to nursing homes. Even Father D'Agostino was helping them. "Lucia," the priest had told her, "you'd have company there."

This Maria from the laundry had a child but no husband. She smiled at Lucia, then peered down into the glass case.

"Miss Mendez needs to ask you a favor," the baker said.

Lucia removed her leather gloves and put them into her purse. "A favor?"

"My little girl," Maria said. "Today is her birthday. She's seven years old today."

"You must know little Teresa," Lorenzo said.

"Yes," Lucia said. She had indeed seen the child, out with her friends tearing up the vegetable gardens in the backyards.

"And I was so busy today at the laundry, so busy, all day long there was a line, and I couldn't get out to buy her a birthday cake."

"Yes." Lucia remembered that it had taken her two days to fix the stakes for her tomato plants.

"Let me explain," Lorenzo said. "Miss Mendez needs a cake and I have none left, except yours. I told her that you were my best customer, and of course we'd have to wait and ask you."

"All the other bakeries are closed," Maria said. "It's my little girl's birthday."

Lucia's hands began to shake. She remembered what the doctor had said about getting angry; but this was too much. "Every week I buy my cake. For how many years? And now this *muli* comes in and you just give it away?"

"Lucy." Lorenzo held out his hands like a little boy. "Don't get angry. Please, Lucy."

"No. Not Lucy." She tapped her chest with her finger. "Lucia."

"Lucy, please," he said.

"No 'Please, Lucy.' No parlare Inglese. Italiano."

"I could give you some sugar cookies," he said. "Or some cannolis. I just made them. They're beautiful."

"Once a week I come here and I buy Nico's cake."

Lorenzo tipped his head to the side. He seemed to be about to say something, but then he stopped. He waited another moment.

"Lucia, think of the poor little girl," he said. "It's her birthday."

"Then bake her a cake. You do the favor, if you like her so much."

"Lucia, there's no time." The party was going to begin in a few minutes, he said. Besides, he had already cleaned

61

his equipment and put away his flour and eggs and sugar.

"Lucia," he said, "it's the right thing. Ask yourself, what would Nico do? Or my father?"

"I know what they wouldn't do. They wouldn't forget who their people were. They wouldn't start speaking Spanish for the *mulis*."

She stared at him until he looked away. Outside, the wind had lifted a newspaper from the sidewalk and was pressing the leaves against the front window of the bakery. From somewhere on Common Street came the sound of a car's engine racing. She thought of Nico, how when he lay sick in bed during his last days she had gone outside and asked the children not to make noise and they'd laughed and told her to go on back inside, crazy old lady.

Without looking up, he spoke in a voice that was almost a whisper. "Lucia," he said, "it's just this once."

"No," she said. "No. I want my cake."

Maria began to cry. "Dios mio," she said. "My little girl."

Lorenzo leaned on his hands. "I'm sorry, Miss Mendez."

Maria turned to her. She was sobbing. "It's my daughter's birthday," she said. "How will she forgive me? Don't you have children?"

"I have three children," Lucia said. "And I never forgot their birthdays. I never had to rush out at the last minute."

"I was working," Maria said. "I'm all by myself with Teresa. I have to raise her alone."

"And whose fault is that?" Lucia waved at Lorenzo. "Pronto," she said. "Box up my cake."

Lorenzo eased the cake out of the display case and placed it into a white cardboard pastry box. His hands were soft and white. He drew a length of twine from the dispenser, tied off the box, then snapped his wrists and broke the string from the leader.

Lucia put on her gloves. As she turned for the door Maria took her arm. "I'll beg you," she said. "Please, I'll buy the cake from you. I'll pay you ten dollars."

Lucia pulled her arm free. "I don't want your money."

"Twenty dollars, then." She pulled a folded bill from the pocket of her dress and placed it in Lucia's hand. "Please, Mrs. Ronsavelli, take it."

Lucia tried to push the bill back into her hands, but Maria curled her fingers into fists and began to cry. "You can't do this," she said.

Lucia threw the crumpled bill to the floor and opened the door. Maria fell to her knees and picked up the bill. "You witch!" she screamed. "Puta! Whore!"

Lucia did not look back. She moved slowly down Newbury Street, being careful to avoid the spots of ice. What did that laundry girl, or even Lorenzo, understand about her? What did they know about devotion?

From the alley behind her building she heard the screaming, a terrible choked wail that rang from the street and into the alley and echoed off the walls and trash cans. She imagined Maria the laundress stumbling home to her daughter, and she imagined the red, contorted face of the little girl when her friends arrived and there was no cake.

Still, what would they know about suffering, even then? They would know nothing. The light was poor in the staircase, and she held the railing with her free hand. After each step she paused; she let the flicker of pain ease from her hips, then lifted again.

Inside the kitchen she raised the glass cover and took out last week's cake. The air that had been under the glass smelled sweet and ripe. The cake had not been touched; it might have been a clay model of the new one. As she carried it to the trash, tips of chocolate frosting broke off and scattered on the floor like shards of pottery.

She swept up the pieces, washed the smudges of frosting from the cake stand with a sponge, then opened the bakery box, removed the new cake and put it under the glass cover. It was dark outside, and in the hills around the city the lights in the windows of hundreds of houses glowed like the tiny white bulbs in the branches of a Christmas tree. She thought of her children; they were up in those hills, eating dinner with their own children – those little light-skinned boys and girls who shrank from their nana's hugs, kept their jackets on, and whispered to each other until it was time to leave. It was cold near the window; she shivered and stepped away.

She sat at the kitchen table, beneath the photos of Nico and the children. She looked at the door, wishing, as she did each time, that there might be a knock, or that it might just swing open, and one of them, just one of them, might be there.

Lynda Sexson
(Born in Washington, 1952)

I wasn't able to turn up much information on Lynda Sexson's background. Bibliographical sources list two story collections: *Margaret of the Imperfections* (1988) and *Hamlet's Planets: Parables* (1997). Sexson herself is better known as a writer of several books on New Age theology than as a creator of fiction. She is Professor of Humanities at Montana State University.

"Turning" I found in a collection of short-shorts called *Sudden Fiction*, which I translated into Japanese back in 1994. It is a very weird piece. Needless to say, I, too, would like to have a tail if possible.

Turning

BY LYNDA SEXSON

Three elderly ladies, elegantly turned with jewels on their elongated necks, helped one another to hobble from the taxi to the walk. They came toward the house, their white curled heads nodding, anticipated by the little boy watching from behind the curtain. They looked like a motion picture of three swans gliding and bobbing on a pale lake, but caught in a faulty, halting projector that was chewing up the frames of their finale. It was as though these fine creatures could not be crippled; it was merely the illusion of a flawed presentation of them.

Inside the house they settled into Queen Anne chairs; prim but for their knees which would no longer stick together, they looked like great water birds, forced not only onto dry land but into human forms that did not suit them. The little boy pushed his trucks on the carpet near them, making highway sound effects for their entertainment. He peeked into the darkness under their skirts, which was like looking into his View Master without the reels. They turned their heads from side to side examining the boy, like birds who have an eye to each hemisphere.

The boy's mother brought out a decorated cake with four candles, bone china cups for the tea, and a glass of milk with a strawberry in it.

"Why, this cake says 'Robert'; the cake has the same name as you," said the first old lady to the boy.

He giggled and fell back on the carpet. "No," he shrieked, "it's my birthday, Louise Dear." He followed religiously their pet names for one another, pronouncing them with formality and deference. They were Louise Dear, Olivia Sweet, and Ruth Love. Every time he said those names it gave them rare little reverberations of pleasure in their old flesh, like spreading circles on the surface of water.

"Why then," said Ruth, "this pretty box must be for you. It says, 'Happy Birthday.'" Robert shredded the wrapping paper and found a shirt bearing an appliqued lion's face with a yarn mane on the front and a cloth tail attached to the back. Robert put it on over his other shirt. He got the buttons wrong; he watched Ruth's fingers work to correct his carelessness. Her knobby fingers looked like bleached, brittle twigs. Robert wondered if they could push the buttons through, not realizing that the lion had been crafted by those same fingers.

His mother lit the candles, the ladies sang, "Happy Birthday, Dear Robert" like the air rushing from leaky organs. Olivia gave him a package of crayons that willfully changed colors as they were used. Robert drew a picture of them on the large drawing paper that accompanied the crayons. The ladies smiled to see themselves emerge as armless, floating shapes, with stick fingers at the sides of ruffled heads, each finished with a distinct and careful navel. He gave the drawing to Olivia.

"We never expected to *receive* a beautiful present on

your birthday," she thanked him. They passed the drawing around and cooed at it.

Louise gave him a package with so many bows it looked like a little animal. Robert chose to keep it as it was, not to look inside yet. The ladies laughed and winked.

He served them cake which they faced as birds would face seeds and crumbs smeared with sticky frosting. Robert waited until they politely abandoned the cake; he leaned into Olivia Sweet's lap, wadding her silky dress into his moist fists, "Let's have a story now." His mother gathered the dishes and left them to their ceremonies.

"This is the story," she said vaguely, "of 'The Emperor Who Had No Skin.'"

"No clothes," corrected Louise.

"No flesh," agreed Ruth.

Olivia's way with stories was to take a great solid wall of a story and knock a chink in it with one word, making it possible and necessary to peer through the chink to the other side. Her story, then, was already told; the chink in the old story was itself the new one. They had only now to find it out by playing it out.

"Once upon a time," she said, "there was an Emperor who had no skin. He looked like ivory carvings and cream-coloured satin cushions all laced together with fine red and blue threads. The Emperor would have been happy but for two things: he wondered why he, alone, had no skin, and he longed for a wife. As he was very rich, very wise, and extremely handsome (the other ladies arched their eyebrows), he came to realize that he himself was a riddle. So he said, whatever princess should answer his riddle should become his wife. At last, a beautiful princess with golden hair and a blue brocaded gown came to his palace . . ."

"And," Louise took up, "she said to the King, 'I have woven a skin for you from my own golden hair, just pull it tightly at the top, once you're in, by this green cord I plaited from the vines that cling to the church walls. For the riddle of your skin is that it must embrace you like a loving wife and find you like a vine finding its way to a tower.'. . ."

Olivia, who knew that stories if not tended could trickle away, broke in harshly, "But the Emperor tried on the skin and knotted the cord and looked in the mirror. He said, 'I look like a mesh bag of nuts and oranges tied with a shoestring in this skin.' He tore it from himself and the princess left weeping."

Louise blinked several times in the silence until Ruth said excitedly, discreetly dabbing at the bit of saliva escaping the corner of her painted mouth, "But another beautiful princess came to the Emperor and told him that she understood his riddle. To be without his skin, she explained, was to be closer to the world and yet without skin was to never feel its petty pricks and pains. And this princess," said Ruth triumphantly, "rolled off her skin like removing a silk stocking, so that she could be like the Emperor and become his bride . . ."

"Yes," Olivia intervened, "and spilled herself out on to the Emperor's royal carpet. It took twenty royal maids twenty days, picking her up and removing her by the thimblesfull."

Louise and Ruth looked at Olivia. Robert, hearing only the story told but not noticing the story between the tellers, said, "Another princess came."

"Yes," Olivia said, "tell us, Robert, about this princess."

"This princess," said Robert, "was red and blue and green and beautiful, and said to the King, 'I'm going to give you a good skin to wear.' And she took off the skin of her best and favorite and big dog and gave it to the King. The dog died but the King said, 'I like this skin because it is fluffy and because it gives me a tail to wag.' And he did."

"But Robert," said Louise, "that doesn't answer the riddle."

"Oh, but it does," said Olivia, to Robert's relief. They all waited for her to continue. At last she said, "You tell us, Robert." The other ladies knew then that the story had turned to one that Olivia could not swim.

"Well," said Robert, "You know, Olivia Sweet, the riddle is that animals have good skins and people would like tails."

"There you have it," said Olivia.

"But," complained Ruth, "*why* was the Emperor without a skin in the first place? That's part of the riddle."

"So we could find him one," said Robert confidently.

"Insufficient, Robert," said Olivia, and he sensed that she meant for him to say more.

"So he could look at the inside of himself before he got married to a princess?" he asked.

"Excellent!" exclaimed Olivia, and seemed about to soar into the air. "I didn't know the answer to that riddle myself," she confided, and the other two applauded the boy.

"Don't ever forget," said Louise, "to look at the inside of yourself before you marry a princess."

"And," said Robert, unable to stop the momentum of his success, "if you wait a long time for a skin you get one with a tail." They laughed and petted him, but he perceived that his last answer was not as good as his former one. He wondered why, as he himself would trade off a dozen princesses for one tail.

The ladies rose to leave. He kissed them on their thin, powdered cheeks and felt how their skins didn't quite fit them and wondered. As Olivia kissed him she said, "Don't ever, Robert, look for morals after you find out riddles."

Squeezed into their taxi, they looked like large fowl stuffed into a crate for market. They waved their white gloves at the house toward the space pulled in the curtain.

David Foster Wallace
(Born in New York State, 1962)

Wallace is among the most talked-about American writers of his generation. Having started writing under the influence of such novelists as Thomas Pynchon and Don DeLillo, Wallace is continually stirring up the literary world with the challenging style and content of his work. His prose can often seem difficult rather than beautiful. Still, it is never deliberately obscure and, as one might expect from a maths graduate, Wallace uses language with stunning precision and coherence, linking each word organically with the next. As long as you can follow his rules (that is, if you can make the decision to follow his rules), the initial sense of unfamiliarity dissipates with relative ease.

This is especially the case in a story like "Forever Overhead", which minutely describes every psychological variation experienced by a boy at each stage as he climbs up the high diving board and finally dives into the pool. Wallace's sequentially sensual prose functions to great effect. The result is a mysterious mixture of the cool and the tender.

Forever Overhead

BY DAVID FOSTER WALLACE

Happy Birthday. Your thirteenth is important. Maybe your first really public day. Your thirteenth is the chance for people to recognize that important things are happening to you.

Things have been happening to you for the past half year. You have seven hairs in your left armpit now. Twelve in your right. Hard dangerous spirals of brittle black hair. Crunchy, animal hair. There are now more of the hard curled hairs around your privates than you can count without losing track. Other things. Your voice is rich and scratchy and moves between octaves without any warning. Your face has begun to get shiny when you don't wash it. And two weeks of a deep and frightening ache this past spring left you with something dropped down from inside: your sack is now full and vulnerable, a commodity to be protected. Hefted and strapped in tight supporters that stripe your buttocks red. You have grown into a new fragility.

And dreams. For months there have been dreams like nothing before: moist and busy and distant, full of yielding curves, frantic pistons, warmth and a great falling; and you have awakened through fluttering lids to a rush and a gush and a toe-curling scalp-snapping jolt of feeling from an inside deeper than you knew you had, spasms of a deep sweet hurt, the streetlights through your window blinds cracking into sharp stars against the black bedroom ceiling, and on you a dense white jam that lisps between legs, trickles and sticks, cools on you, hardens and clears until there is nothing but gnarled knots of pale solid animal hair in the morning shower, and in the wet tangle a clean sweet smell you can't believe comes from anything you made inside you.

The smell is, more than anything, like this swimming pool: a bleached sweet salt, a flower with chemical petals. The pool has a strong clear blue smell, though you know the smell is never as strong when you are actually in the blue water, as you are now, all swum out, resting back along the shallow end, the hip-high water lapping at where it's all changed.

Around the deck of this old public pool on the western edge of Tucson is a Cyclone fence the color of pewter, decorated with a bright tangle of locked bicycles. Beyond this a hot black parking lot full of white lines and glittering cars. A dull field of dry grass and hard weeds, old dandelions' downy heads exploding and snowing up in a rising wind. And past all this, reddened by a round slow September sun, are mountains, jagged, their tops' sharp angles darkening into definition against a deep red tired light. Against the red their sharp connected tops form a spiked line, an EKG of the dying day.

The clouds are taking on color by the rim of the sky.

The water is spangles off soft blue, five-o'clock warm, and the pool's smell, like the other smell, connects with a chemical haze inside you, an interior dimness that bends light to its own ends, softens the difference between what leaves off and what begins.

Your party is tonight. This afternoon, on your birthday, you have asked to come to the pool. You wanted to come alone, but a birthday is a family day, your family wants to be with you. This is nice, and you can't talk about why you wanted to come alone, and really truly maybe you didn't want to come alone, so they are here. Sunning. Both your parents sun. Their deck chairs have been marking time all afternoon, rotating, tracking the sun's curve across a desert sky heated to an eggy film. Your sister plays Marco Polo near you in the shallows with a group of thin girls from her grade. She is being blind now, her Marco's being Polo'd. She is shut-eyed and twirling to different cries, spinning at the hub of a wheel of shrill girls in bathing caps. Her cap has raised rubber flowers. There are limp old pink petals that shake as she lunges at blind sound.

There at the other end of the pool is the diving tank and the high board's tower. Back on the deck behind is the SN CK BAR, and on either side, bolted above the cement entrances to dark wet showers and lockers, are gray metal bullhorn speakers that send out the pool's radio music, the jangle flat and tinny thin.

Your family likes you. You are bright and quiet, respect-ful to elders – though you are not without spine. You are largely good. You look out for your little sister. You are her ally. You were six when she was zero and you had the mumps when they brought her home in a very soft yellow blanket; you kissed her hello on her feet out of concern that she not catch your mumps. Your parents say that this augured well. That it set the tone. They now feel they were right. In all things they are proud of you, satisfied, and they have retreated to the warm distance from which pride and satisfaction travel. You all get along well.

Happy Birthday. It is a big day, big as the roof of the whole southwest sky. You have thought it over. There is the high board. They will want to leave soon. Climb out and do the thing.

Shake off the blue clean. You're half-bleached, loose and soft, tenderized, pads of fingers wrinkled. The mist of the pool's too clean smell is in your eyes; it breaks light into gentle color. Knock your head with the heel of your hand. One side has a flabby echo. Cock your head to the side and hop – sudden heat in your ear, delicious and brain-warmed water turns cold on the nautilus of your ear's outside. You can hear harder tinnier music, closer shouts, much movement in much water.

The pool is crowded for this late. Here are thin children, hairy animal men. Disproportionate boys, all necks and legs and knobby joints, shallow-chested, vaguely bird-like. Like you. Here are old people moving tentatively through shallows on stick legs, feeling at the water with their hands, out of every element at once.

And girl-women, women, curved like instruments or fruit, skin burnished brown-bright, suit tops held by delicate knots of fragile colored string against the pull of mysterious weights, suit bottoms riding low over the gentle juts of hips totally unlike your own, immoderate swells and swivels that melt in light into a surrounding space that cups and accommodates the soft curves as things precious. You almost understand.

The pool is a system of movement. Here now there are: laps, splash fights, divers, corner tag, cannonballs, Sharks and Minnows, high fallings, Marco Polo (your sister still It, halfway to tears, too long to be It, the game teetering on the edge of cruelty, not your business to save or embarrass). Two clean little bright-white boys caped in cotton towels run along the poolside until the guard stops them dead with a shout through his bullhorn. The guard is brown as a tree, blond hair in a vertical line on his stomach, his head in a jungle explorer hat, his nose a white triangle of cream. A girl has an arm around a leg of his little tower. He's bored.

Get out now and go past your parents, who are sunning and reading, not looking up. Forget your towel. Stopping for the towel means talking and talking means thinking. You have decided being scared is caused mostly by thinking. Go right by, toward the tank at the deep end. Over the tank is a great iron tower of dirty white. A board protrudes from the top of the tower like a tongue. The pool's concrete deck is rough and hot against your bleached feet. Each of your footprints is thinner and fainter. Each shrinks behind you on the hot stone and disappears.

Lines of plastic wieners bob around the tank, which is entirely its own thing, empty of the rest of the pool's convulsive ballet of heads and arms. The tank is blue as energy, small and deep and perfectly square, flanked by lap lanes and SN CK BAR and rough hot deck and the bent late shadow of the tower and board. The tank is quiet and still and healed smooth between fallings.

There is a rhythm to it. Like breathing. Like a machine. The line for the board curves back from the tower's ladder. The line moves in its curve, straightens as it nears the ladder. One by one, people reach the ladder and climb. One by one, spaced by the beat of hearts, they reach the tongue of the board at the top. And once on the board, they pause, each exactly the same tiny heartbeat pause. And their legs take them to the end, where they all give the same sort of stomping hop, arms curving out as if to describe something circular, total; they come down heavy on the edge of the board and make it throw them up and out.

It's a swooping machine, lines of stuttered movement in a sweet late bleach mist. You can watch from the deck as they hit the cold blue sheet of the tank. Each fall makes a white that plumes and falls into itself and spreads and fizzes. Then blue clean comes up in the middle of the white and spreads like pudding, making it all new. The tank heals itself. Three times as you go by.

You are in line. Look around. Look bored. Few talk in the line. Everyone seems by himself. Most look at the ladder, look bored. You almost all have crossed arms, chilled by a late dry rising wind on the constellations of blue-clean chlorine beads that cover your backs and shoulders. It seems impossible that everybody could really be this bored. Beside you is the edge of the tower's shadow, the tilted black tongue of the board's image. The system of shadow is huge, long, off to the side, joined to the tower's base at a sharp late angle.

Almost everyone in line for the board watches the ladder. Older boys watch older girls' bottoms as they go up. The bottoms are in soft thin cloth, tight nylon stretch. The good bottoms move up on the ladder like pendulums in liquid, a gentle uncrackable code. The girls' legs make you think of deer. Look bored.

Look out past it. Look across. You can see so well. Your mother is in her deck chair, reading, squinting, her face tilted up to get light on her cheeks. She hasn't looked to see where you are. She sips something sweet out of a bright can. Your father is on his big stomach, back like the hint of a hump of a whale, shoulders curling with animal spirals, skin oiled and soaked red-brown with too much sun. Your towel is hanging off your chair and a corner of the cloth now moves – your mother hit it as she waved away a sweat bee that likes what she has in the can. The bee is back right away, seeming to hang motionless over the can in a sweet blur. Your towel is one big face of Yogi Bear.

At some point there has gotten to be more line behind you than in front of you. Now no one in front except three on the slender ladder. The woman right before you is on the low rungs, looking up, wearing a tight black nylon suit that is all one piece. She climbs. From above there is a rumble, then a great falling, then a plume and the tank reheals. Now two on the ladder. The pool rules say one on the ladder at a time, but the guard never shouts about it. The guard makes the real rules by shouting or not shouting.

This woman above you should not wear a suit as tight as the suit she is wearing. She is as old as your mother, and as big. She is too big and too white. Her suit is full of her. The backs of her thighs are squeezed by the suit and look like cheese. Her legs have abrupt little squiggles of cold blue shattered vein under the white skin, as if something were broken, hurt, in her legs. Her legs look like they hurt to be squeezed, full of curled Arabic lines of cold broken blue. Her legs make you feel like your own legs hurt.

The rungs are very thin. It's unexpected. Thin round iron rungs laced in slick wet Safe-T felt. You taste metal from the smell of wet iron in shadow. Each rung presses into the bottoms of your feet and dents them. The dents feel deep and they hurt. You feel heavy. How the big woman over you must feel. The handrails along the ladder's sides are also very thin. It's like you might not hold on. You've got to hope the woman holds on, too. And of course it looked like fewer rungs from far away. You are not stupid.

Get halfway up, up in the open, big woman placed above you, a solid bald muscular man on the ladder underneath your feet. The board is still high overhead, invisible from here. But it rumbles and makes a heavy flapping sound, and a boy you can see for a few contained feet through the thin rungs falls in a flash of a line, a knee held to his chest, doing a splasher. There is a huge exclamation point of foam up into your field of sight, then scattered claps into a great fizzing. Then the silent sound of the tank healing to new blue all over again.

More thin rungs. Hold on tight. The radio is loudest

here, one speaker at ear-level over a concrete locker room entrance. A cool dank whiff of the locker room inside. Grab the iron bars tight and twist and look down behind you and you can see people buying snacks and refreshments below. You can see down into it: the clean white top of the vendor's cap, tubs of ice cream, steaming brass freezers, scuba tanks of soft drink syrup, snakes of soda hose, bulging boxes of salty popcorn kept hot in the sun. Now that you're overhead you can see the whole thing.

There's wind. It's windier the higher you get. The wind is thin; through the shadow it's cold on your wet skin. On the ladder in the shadow your skin looks very white. The wind makes a thin whistle in your ears. Four more rungs to the top of the tower. The rungs hurt your feet. They are thin and let you know just how much you weigh. You have real weight on the ladder. The ground wants you back.

Now you can see just over the top of the ladder. You can see the board. The woman is there. There are two ridges of red, hurt-looking callus on the backs of her ankles. She stands at the start of the board, your eyes on her ankles. Now you're up above the tower's shadow. The solid man under you is looking through the rungs into the contained space the woman's fall will pass through.

She pauses for just that beat of a pause. There's nothing slow about it at all. It makes you cold. In no time she's at the end of the board, up, down on it, it bends low like it doesn't want her. Then it nods and flaps and throws her violently up and out, her arms opening out to inscribe that circle, and gone. She disappears in a dark blink. And there's time before you hear the hit below.

Listen. It does not seem good, the way she disappears into a time that passes before she sounds. Like a stone down a well. But you think she did not think so. She was part of a rhythm that excludes thinking. And now you have made yourself part of it, too. The rhythm seems blind. Like ants. Like a machine.

You decide this needs to be thought about. It may, after all, be all right to do something scary without thinking, but not when the scariness is the not thinking itself. Not when not thinking turns out to be wrong. At some point the wrongnesses have piled up blind: pretend-boredom, weight, thin rungs, hurt feet, space cut into laddered parts that melt together only in a disappearance that takes time. The wind on the ladder not what anyone would have expected. The way the board protrudes from shadow into light and you can't see past the end. When it all turns out to be different you should get to think. It should be required.

The ladder is full beneath you. Stacked up, everyone a few rungs apart. The ladder is fed by a solid line that stretches back and curves into the dark of the tower's canted shadow. People's arms are crossed in the line. Those on the ladder's feet hurt and they are all looking up. It is a machine that moves only forward.

Climb up onto the tower's tongue. The board turns out to be long. As long as the time you stand there. Time slows. It thickens around you as your heart gets more and more beats out of every second, every movement in the system of the pool below.

The board is long. From where you stand it seems to stretch off into nothing. It's going to send you someplace which its own length keeps you from seeing, which seems wrong to submit to without even thinking.

Looked at another way, the same board is just a long thin flat thing covered with a rough white plastic stuff. The white surface is very rough and is freckled and lined with a pale watered red that is nevertheless still red and not yet pink – drops of old pool water that are catching the light of the late sun over sharp mountains. The rough white stuff of the board is wet. And cold. Your feet are hurt from the thin rungs and have a great ability to feel. They feel your weight. There are handrails running above the beginning of the board. They are not like the ladder's handrails just were. They are thick and set very low, so you almost have to bend over to hold on to them. They are just for show, no one holds them. Holding on takes time and alters the rhythm of the machine.

It is a long cold rough white plastic or fiberglass board, veined with the sad near-pink color of bad candy.

But at the end of the white board, the edge, where you'll come down with your weight to make it send you off, there are two areas of darkness. Two flat shadows in the broad light. Two vague black ovals. The end of the board has two dirty spots.

They are from all the people who've gone before you. Your feet as you stand here are tender and dented, hurt by the rough wet surface, and you see that the two dark spots are from people's skin. They are skin abraded from feet by the violence of the disappearance of people with real weight. More people than you could count without losing track. The weight and abrasion of their disappearance leaves little bits of soft tender feet behind, bits and shards and curls of skin that dirty and darken and tan as they lie tiny and smeared in the sun at the end of the board. They pile up and get smeared and mixed together. They darken in two circles.

No time is passing outside you at all. It is amazing. The late ballet below is slow motion, the overbroad movements of mimes in blue jelly. If you wanted you could really stay here forever, vibrating inside so fast you float motionless in time, like a bee over something sweet.

But they should clean the board. Anybody who thought about it for even a second would see that they should clean the end of the board of people's skin, of two black collections of what's left of before, spots that from back here look like eyes, like blind and cross-eyed eyes.

Where you are now is still and quiet. Wind radio shouting splashing not here. No time and no real sound but your blood squeaking in your head.

Overhead here means sight and smell. The smells are intimate, newly clear. The smell of bleach's special flower, but out of it other things rise to you like a weed's seeded snow. You smell deep yellow popcorn. Sweet tan oil like hot coconut. Either hot dogs or corn dogs. A thin cruel hint of very dark Pepsi in paper cups. And the special smell of tons of water coming off tons of skin, rising like steam off a new bath. Animal heat. From overhead it is more real than anything.

Look at it. You can see the whole complicated thing, blue and white and brown and white, soaked in a watery spangle of deepening red. Everybody. This is what people call a view. And you knew that from below you wouldn't look nearly so high overhead. You see now how high overhead you are. You knew from down there no one could tell.

He says it behind you, his eyes on your ankles, the solid bald man, Hey kid. They want to know. Do your plans up here involve the whole day or what exactly is the story. Hey kid are you okay.

There's been time this whole time. You can't kill time with your heart. Everything takes time. Bees have to move very fast to stay still.

Hey kid he says Hey kid are you okay.

Metal flowers bloom on your tongue. No more time for thinking. Now that there is time you don't have time.

Hey.

Slowly now, out across everything, there's a watching that spreads like hit water's rings. Watch it spread out from the ladder. Your sighted sister and her thin white pack, pointing. Your mother looks to the shallows where you used to be, then makes a visor of her hand. The whale stirs and jiggles. The guard looks up, the girl around his leg looks up, he reaches for his horn.

Forever below is rough deck, snacks, thin metal music, down where you once used to be; the line is solid and has no reverse gear; and the water, of course, is only soft when you're inside it. Look down. Now it moves in the sun, full of hard coins of light that shimmer red as they stretch away into a mist that is your own sweet salt. The coins crack into new moons, long shards of light from the hearts of sad stars. The square tank is a cold blue sheet. Cold is just a kind of hard. A kind of blind. You have been taken off guard. Happy Birthday. Did you think it over. Yes and no. Hey kid.

Two black spots, violence, and disappear into a well of time. Height is not the problem. It all changes when you get back down. When you hit, with your weight.

So which is the lie? Hard or soft? Silence or time?

The lie is that it's one or other. A still, floating bee is moving faster than it can think. From overhead the sweetness drives it crazy.

The board will nod and you will go, and eyes of skin can cross blind into a cloud-blotched sky, punctured light emptying behind sharp stone that is forever. That is forever. Step into the skin and disappear.

Hello.

Ethan Canin
(Born in Michigan, 1960)

Hip young writers like Jay McInerney, Bret Easton Ellis and Tama Janowitz danced into the 1980s American literary scene with their original style and tales for their own generation. Ethan Canin was another writer who debuted around this time, but the spotlight never suited this quiet Harvard Medical School student. Canin, too, seemed to differentiate himself from others of his generation when he declared that "You write a truer book when the style is less apparent".

The stories Canin writes could not be called experimental. They draw instead from the orthodox mainstream and at times they can seem somewhat contrived, though never conservative. Everything he writes is quietly, honestly imbued with a supple sense of his individuality. This story is one of his very best. I hope you enjoy it.

Angel of Mercy, Angel of Wrath

BY ETHAN CANIN

On Eleanor Black's 71st birthday a flock of birds flew into her kitchen through a window that she had opened every morning for 40 years. They flew in all at once, without warning or reason, from the ginkgo tree at the corner, where birds had sat every day since President Roosevelt's time. They were huge and dirty and black, the size of cats practically, much larger than she had ever imagined birds. Birds were so small in the sky. In the air, even in the clipped ginkgo 10 yards from the window, they were nothing more than faint dots of color. Now they were in her kitchen, batting against the ceiling and the yellow walls she had just washed a couple of months ago, and their stink and their cries and their frantic knocking wings made it hard for her to breathe.

She sat down and took a water pill. They were screaming like wounded animals, flapping in tight circles around the light fixture so that she got dizzy looking at them. She reached for the phone and pushed the button that automatically dialed her son, who was a doctor.

"Bernard," she said, "there's a flock of crows in the flat."

"It's 5 in the morning, Mom."

"It is? Excuse me, because it's 7 out here. I forgot. But the crows are flying in my kitchen."

"Mother?"

"Yes?"

"Have you been taking all your medicines?"

"Yes, I have."

"Has Dr. Gluck put you on any new ones?"

"No."

"What did you say was the matter?"

"There's a whole flock of crows in the flat."

Bernard didn't say anything.

"I know what you're thinking," she said.

"I'm just making the point that sometimes new medicines can change people's perceptions."

"Do you want to hear them?"

"Yes," he said, "that would be fine. Let me hear them."

She held the receiver up toward the ceiling. The cries were so loud she knew he would pick them up, even long distance.

"Okay?" she said.

"I'll be damned."

"What am I supposed to do?"

"How many are there?"

"I don't know."

"What do you mean, you don't know?"

"They're flying like crazy around the room. How can I count them?"

"Are they attacking you?"

"No, but I want them out anyway."

"How can I get them out from Denver?"

She thought for a second. "I'm not the one who went to Denver."

He breathed out on the phone, loud, like a child. He was chief of the department at Denver General. "I'm just making the point," he said, "that I can't grab a broom in Colorado and get the birds out of your place in New York."

"Whose fault is that?"

"Mom," he said.

"Yes?"

"Call the SPCA. Tell them what happened. They have a department that's for things like this. They'll come out and get rid of them."

"They're big."

"I know," he said. "Don't call 911. That's for emergencies. Call the regular SPCA. Okay?"

"Okay," she said.

He paused. "You can call back later to let us know what happened."

"Okay."

"Okay?"

"Okay." She waited a moment. "Do you want to say anything else?"

"No," he said.

She hung up, and a few seconds later all the birds flew back out the window except for two of them, which flew the other way, through the swinging door that she had left open and into the living room. She followed them in there. One of them was hopping on the bookshelf, but while Eleanor watched, the other one flew straight at the window from the center of the room and collided with the glass. The pane shook, and the bird fell several feet before it righted itself and did the same thing again. For a few moments Eleanor stood watching, and then she went to the kitchen, took the bottle of cream soda out of the refrigerator, and poured herself a glass. Yesterday it had been a hundred degrees out. When she finished, she put the bottle back, sat down again, and dialed 911.

"Emergency," said a woman.

Eleanor didn't say anything.

"911 Emergency."

"There's a flock of crows in my apartment."

"Birds?"

"Yes."

"You have to call the SPCA."

"They're going to break the window."

"Listen," she said, "we're not supposed to give this kind of advice, but all you have to do is move up quietly behind a bird and pick it up. They won't hurt you. I grew up on a farm."

"I grew up here."

"You can do that," she said, "or you can call the SPCA."

She hung up and went back to the living room. One still perched itself on the edge of her bookshelf and sat there, opening and closing its wings, while the other one, the berserk one, flew straight at the front window, smashed into it, fell to the sill, and then took to the air again. Again and again it flew straight at the window, hitting it with a sound like a walnut in a nutcracker, falling to the sill, then flapping crookedly back toward the center of the room to make another run. Already the window had small blotches of bluish feather oil on it. The bird hit it again, fell flapping to the sill, and this time stayed there, perched. Through the window Eleanor noticed that the house across the street from her had been painted green.

"Stay here," she said. "I'm going to open the window."

She took two steps toward the bird, keeping the rest of her body as still as she could, like a hunting dog, moving one leg, pausing, then moving the other. Next to her on the bookshelf the calm bird cocked its head in little jerks – down, up, sideways, down. She advanced toward the window until the berserk one suddenly flew up, smashed against the glass, fell to the sill, flew up again, smashed, and perched once more. She stopped. It stood there. To her horror, Eleanor could see its grotesque pulse through its skin, beating frantically along the wings and the torso as if the whole bird were nothing but a speeding heart. She stood perfectly still for several minutes, watching.

"Hello," she said.

It lifted its wings as though it were going to fly against the window again, but then lowered them.

"My husband was a friend of Franklin Roosevelt's," she said.

The bird didn't move.

"Why can't you be like your friend?" She pointed her chin at the one on the bookshelf, which opened its beak. Inside it the throat was black. She took another step toward the window. Now she was so close to the berserk one that she could see the ruffled, purplish chest-feathers and the yellow ring around its black irises. Its heart still pulsated, but it didn't raise its wings, just cocked its head the way the other one had. She reached her two hands halfway toward it and stopped. "It's my birthday today," she whispered. She waited like that, her hands extended. The bird cocked and retracted its head, then stood still. When it had been still for a while, she reached the rest of the way and touched her hands to both sides of its quivering body.

For a moment, for an extended, odd moment in which the laws of nature didn't seem to hold, for a moment in which she herself felt just the least bit confused, the bird stood still. It was oily and cool, and its askew feathers poked her palms. What she thought about at that second, of all things, was the day her husband, Charles, had come into the living room to announce to her that President Kennedy was going to launch missiles against the Cubans. She had felt the same way when he told her that, as if something had gone slightly wrong with nature that she couldn't quite comprehend, the way right now she couldn't quite comprehend the bird's stillness until suddenly it shrieked and twisted in her hands and flew up into the air.

She stepped back. It circled through the room and smashed into the glass again, this time on the other window next to the bookshelf. The calm bird lighted from its perch, went straight down the hall, and flew into her bedroom. The berserk one righted itself and flew into the glass again, then flapped up and down against it, tapping the wide pane with its wings like a moth. Eleanor went to the front window, but she couldn't open it because the Mexican boy who had painted the apartments last year had broken the latch. She crossed into the kitchen and looked up the number of the SPCA.

A child answered the phone. Eleanor had to think for a second. "I'd like to report two crows in my house," she said.

The child put down the phone, and a moment later a woman came on the line. "I'd like to report two crows in my house," said Eleanor. The woman hung up. Eleanor looked up the number again. This time a man answered. "Society," he said.

"There are two crows in my house," said Eleanor.

"Did they come in a window?"

"I always have that window opened," she answered. "I've had it opened for years with nothing happening."

"Then it's open now?"

"Yes."

"Have you tried getting them out?"

"Yes. I grabbed one the way the police said, but it bit me."

"It bit you?"

"Yes. The police gave me that advice over the phone."

"Did it puncture the skin?"

"It's bleeding a little."

"Where are they now?"

"They're in the living room," she said. "One's in another room."

"All right," he said. "Tell me your address."

When they finished, Eleanor hung up and went into the living room. The berserk one was perched on the sill, looking into the street. She went into the bedroom and had to look around a while before she found the calm one sitting on top of her lamp.

She had lived a long enough life to know there was nothing to be lost from waiting out situations, so she turned out the light in the bedroom, went back into the living room, took the plastic seat cover off the chair President Roosevelt had sat on, and, crossing her arms, sat down on it herself. By now the berserk bird was calm. It stood on the windowsill, and every once in a while it strutted three or four jerky steps up the length of the wood, turned toward her, and bobbed its head. She nodded at it.

The last time the plastic had been off that chair was the day Richard Nixon resigned. Charles had said that Franklin Roosevelt would have liked it that way, so they took the plastic off and sat on it that day and for a few days after, until Charles let some peanuts fall between the cushion and the arm and she got worried and covered it again. After all those years the chair was still firm.

The bird eyed her. Its feet had four claws and were scaly, like the feet on a butcher's chicken. "Get out of here," she said. "Go! Go through the window you came from." She flung her hand out at it, flapped it in front of the chair, but the bird didn't move. She sat back.

When the doorbell rang, she got up and answered on the building intercom. It was the SPCA. When she opened the door to the apartment, she found a young black woman standing there. She was fat, with short, braided hair.

After the woman had introduced herself and stepped inside, Eleanor was surprised to see that the hair on one side of her head was long. She wore overalls and a pink turtleneck.

"Now," she said, "where are those crows you indicated?"

"In the living room," said Eleanor. "He was going to break the glass soon if you didn't get here."

"I got here as soon as I received the call."

"I didn't mean that."

The woman stepped into the living room, swaying slightly on her right leg, which looked partly crippled. The bird hopped from the sill to the sash, then back to the sill. The woman stood motionless with her hands together in front of her watching it. "That's no crow," she said finally. "That's a grackle. That's a rare species here."

"I grew up in New York," said Eleanor.

"So did I." The woman stepped back, turned away from the bird, and began looking at Eleanor's living room. "A crow's a rare species here, too, you know. Some of that particular species gets confused and comes in here from Long Island."

"Poor things."

"Say," said the woman. "Do you have a little soda or something? It's hot out."

"I'll look," said Eleanor. "I heard it was a hundred degrees out yesterday."

Eleanor went into the kitchen. She opened the refrigerator door, stood there, then closed it. "I'm out of everything," she called.

"That's all right."

She filled a glass with water and brought it out to the woman. "There you go," she said.

The woman drank it. "Well," she said. "I think I'll make the capture now."

"It's my birthday today."

"Is that right?"

"Yes, it is."

"How old are you?"

"Eighty-one."

The woman reached behind her, picked up the water glass, and made the gesture of a toast. "Well, happy 81st," she said. She put down the glass and walked over and opened the front window. Then she crouched and approached the bird, which was on the other sill. She stepped slowly, her head tilted to the side and her large arms held in front of her, and when she was a few feet before the window, she bent forward and took the bird into her hands. It flapped a couple of times and then sat still in her grasp while she turned and walked it to the open window, where she let it go and it flew away into the air.

After the woman left, Eleanor put the plastic back on the chair and called her son again. The hospital had to page him, and when he came on the phone he sounded annoyed.

"It was difficult," she said. "The fellow from SPCA had to come out."

"Did he do a decent job?"

"Yes, decent."

"Good," he said. "I'm very pleased."

"It was a rare species," said Eleanor. "He had to use a metal-handled capturing device. It was a long set of tongs with hinges."

"Good, I'm very pleased."

"Are you at work?"

"Yes, I am."

"Okay, then."

"Okay."

"Is there anything else?"

"No," he said. "That's it."

A while after they hung up, the doorbell rang. It was the SPCA woman again, and when Eleanor let her upstairs, she found her standing in the hall with a bunch of carnations wrapped in newspaper. "Here," she said. "Happy birthday from the SPCA."

"Oh my," said Eleanor. For a moment she thought she was going to cry. "They're very elegant."

The woman stepped into the apartment. "I just thought you were a nice lady."

"Why, thank you very much." She took them and laid them down on the hall vanity. "Would you like a cup of tea?"

"No, thanks. I just wanted to bring them up. I've got more calls to take care of."

"Would you like some more water?"

"That's all right," said the woman. She smiled and touched Eleanor on the shoulder, then turned and went back downstairs.

Eleanor closed the door and unwrapped the flowers. She looked closely at their stems for signs that they were a few days old, but could find none. The ends were unswollen and cleanly clipped at an angle. She brought them into the kitchen, washed out a vase, and set them in it. Then she poured herself half a glass of cream soda. When she was finished, she went into the bedroom, took a sheet of paper from the drawer in the bedside table, and began a letter.

Dear President Bush:

I am a friend of President Roosevelt's writing you on my eightieth birthday on the subject of a rare species that came into my life without warning today and that needs help from a man such as yourself

She sat up straight and examined the letter. The handwriting got smaller at the end of each line, so she put the paper aside and took out a new sheet. At that moment the calm bird flew down and perched on the end of the table. Eleanor jerked back and stood away from the chair. "Oh," she said, and touched her heart. "Of course."

Then she patted her hair with both hands and sat down again. The bird tilted its head to look at her. Eleanor looked back. Its coat was black, but she could see an iridescent rainbow in the chest feathers. It strutted a couple of steps toward her, flicking its head left, right, forward. Its eyes were dark.

She put out her hand, leaned a little bit, and, moving her head steadily and slowly, touched the feathers once and withdrew. The bird hopped and opened its wings. She sat back and watched it. Sitting there, she knew that it probably didn't mean anything. She was just a woman in an apartment, and it was just a bird that had wandered in. It was too bad they couldn't talk to each other. She would have liked to know how old the bird was, and what it was like to have lived in the sky.

Andrea Lee
(Born in Philadelphia, 1953)

After taking an M.A. at Harvard, Andrea Lee became a staff writer for the *New Yorker* while energetically contributing stories and non-fiction to a variety of magazines. She was still in her twenties when her first book, *Russian Journal*, was nominated for the National Book Award. Later she fell in love with and married an Italian aristocrat, had two children and now lives in Turin.

This quick outline of Lee's career is itself enough to elicit a sigh, but in addition she is a woman of remarkable beauty. I myself was fortunate enough to meet her – however briefly – in New York not long ago and found her to be slim and elegant, with an air of sophisticated intelligence. I think I can see why one critic has written, "She may be one of the only writers whose actual life might be more interesting than the fictional ones she creates for her characters" (Jenny Lee). This story, "The Birthday Present", appears in Lee's most recent collection, *Interesting Women* (2002).

The Birthday Present

BY ANDREA LEE

A cellular phone is ringing, somewhere in Milan. Ariel knows that much. Or does she? The phone could be trilling its electronic morsel of Mozart or Bacharach in a big vulgar villa with guard dogs and closed-circuit cameras on the bosky shores of Lake Como. Or in an overpriced hotel suite in Portofino. Or why not in the Aeolian Islands, or on Ischia, or Sardinia? It's late September, and all over the Mediterranean the yachts of politicians and arms manufacturers and pan-Slavic gangsters are still snuggled side by side in the indulgent golden light of harbors where the calendars of the toiling masses mean nothing. The truth is that the phone could be ringing anywhere in the world where there are rich men.

But Ariel prefers to envision Milan, which is the city nearest the Brianza countryside, where she lives with her family in a restored farmhouse. And she tries hard to imagine the tiny phone lying on a table in an apartment not unlike the one she shared fifteen years ago in Washington with a couple of other girls who were seniors at Georgetown. The next step up from a dorm, that is – like a set for sitcom about young professionals whose sex lives, though kinky, have an endearing adolescent gaucheness. It would be too disturbing to think that she is telephoning a bastion of contemporary Milanese luxury, like the apartments of some of her nouveau-riche friends: gleaming marble, bespoke mosaics, boiserie stripped from defunct châteaux, a dispiriting sense of fresh money spread around like butter on toast.

Hmmm – and if it *were* a place like that? There would be, she supposes, professional modifications. Mirrors: that went without saying, as did a bed the size of a hand-ball court, with a nutria cover and conveniently installed handcuffs. Perhaps a small dungeon off the dressing room? At any rate, a bathroom with Moroccan hammam fixtures and a bidet made from an antique baptismal font. Acres of closets, with garter belts and crotchless panties folded and stacked with fetishistic perfection. And boxes of specialty condoms, divided, perhaps, by design and flavor. Are they ordered by the gross? From a catalog? But now Ariel retrieves her thoughts, because someone picks up the phone.

"*Pronto?*" The voice is young and friendly and hasty.

"Is this Beba?" Ariel asks in her correct but heavy Italian, from which she has never attempted to erase the American accent.

"Yes," says the voice, with a merry air of haste.

"I'm a friend of Falvio Costaldo's and he told me that you and your friend – your colleague – might be interested in spending an evening with my husband. It's a birthday present."

When a marriage lingers at a certain stage – the not uncommon plateau where the two people involved have nothing to say to each other – it is sometimes still possible for them to live well together. To perform generous acts that do not, exactly, signal desperation. Flavio hadn't meant to inspire action when he suggested that Ariel give her husband, Roberto, *"una fanciulla"* – a young girl – for his fifty-fifth birthday. He'd meant only to irritate, as usual. Flavio is Roberto's best friend, a sixty-year-old Calabrian film producer who five or six years ago gave up trying to seduce Ariel, and settled for the alternative intimacy of tormenting her subtly whenever they meet. Ariel is a tall, fresh-faced woman of thirty-seven, an officer's child who grew up on army bases around the world, and whose classic American beauty has an air of crisp serviceability that – she is well aware – is a major flaw: in airports, she is sometimes accosted by travelers who are convinced that she is there in a professional capacity. She is always patient at parties when the inevitable pedant expounds on how unsuitable it is for a tall, rather slow-moving beauty to bear the name of the most volatile of spirits. Her own opinion – resolutely unvoiced, like so many of her thoughts – is that, besides being ethereal, Shakespeare's Ariel was mainly competent and faithful. As she herself is by nature: a rarity anywhere in the world, but particularly in Italy. She is the ideal wife – second wife – for Robert, who is an old-fashioned domestic tyrant. And she is the perfect victim for Flavio. When he made the suggestion, they were sitting in the garden of his fourth wife's sprawling modern villa in a gated community near Como, and both of their spouses were off at the other end of the terrace, looking at samples of glass brick. But Ariel threw him handily off balance by laughing and taking up the idea. As she did so, she thought of how much affection she'd come to feel for good old Flavio since her early days in Italy, when she'd reserved for him the ritual loathing of a new wife for her husband's best friend. Nowadays she was a compassionate observer of his dawning old age and its accoutrements, the karmic doom of any superannuated playboy: tinted aviator bifocals and reptilian complexion; a rich, tyrannical wife who imposed a strict diet of fidelity and bland foods; a little brown address book full of famous pals who no longer phoned. That afternoon, Ariel for the first time had the satisfaction of watching his composure crumble when she asked him sweetly to get her the number of the best call girl in Milan.

"You're not serious," he sputtered. "Ariel, cara, you've known me long enough to know I was joking. You aren't—"

"Don't go into that nice-girl, bad-girl Latin thing, Flavio. It's a little dated, even for you."

"I was going to say only that you aren't an Italian wife, and there are nuances you'll never understand, even if you live here for a hundred years."

"Oh, please, spare me the anthropology," said Ariel. It was pleasant to have rattled Flavio to this extent. The idea of the *fanciulla*, to which she had agreed on a mischievous impulse unusual for her, suddenly grew more concrete. "Just get me the number."

Flavio was silent for a few minutes, his fat, sunspeckled hands wreathing his glass of *limoncello*. "You're still sleeping together?" he asked suddenly. "Is it all right?"

"Yes, and yes."

"*Allora, che diavolo stai facendo?* What the hell are you doing? He's faithful to you, you know. It's an incredible thing for such a womanizer; you know about his first marriage. With you there have been a few little lapses, but nothing important."

Ariel nodded, not even the slightest bit offended. She knew about those lapses, had long before factored them into her expectations about the perpetual foreign life she had chosen. Nothing he said, however, could distract her from her purpose.

Flavio sighed and cast his eyes heavenward. "*Va bene;* Okay. But you have to be very careful," he said, shooting a glance down the terrace at his ever-vigilant wife, with her gold sandals and anorexic body. After a minute, he added cryptically, "Well, at least you're Catholic. That's something."

So, thanks to Flavio's little brown book, Ariel is now talking to Beba. Beba – a toddler's nickname. Ex-model in her twenties. Brazilian, but not a transsexual. Tall. Dark. Works in tandem with a Russian blonde. "The two of them are so gorgeous that when you see them it's as if you have entered another sphere, a paradise where everything is simple and divine," said Flavio, waxing lyrical during the series of planning phone calls he and Ariel shared, cozy conversations that made his wife suspicious and gave him the renewed pleasure of annoying Ariel. "The real danger is that Roberto might fall in love with one of them," he remarked airily, during one of their chats. "No, probably not – he's too stingy."

In contrast, it is easy talking to Beba. "How many men?" Beba asks, as matter-of-factly as a caterer. There is a secret happiness in her voice that tempts Ariel to investigate, to talk more than she normally would. It is an impulse she struggles to control. She knows from magazine articles that, like everyone else, prostitutes simply want to get their work done without a fuss.

"Just my husband," Ariel says, feeling a calm boldness settle over her.

"And you?"

Flavio has said that Beba is a favorite among rich Milanese ladies who are fond of extracurricular romps. Like the unlisted addresses where they buy their cashmere and have their abortions, she is top-of-the-line and highly private. Flavio urged Ariel to participate and gave a knowing chuckle when she refused. The chuckle meant that, like everyone else, he thinks Ariel is a prude. She isn't – though the fact is obscured by her fatal air of efficiency, by her skill at writing out place cards, making homemade tagliatelle better than her Italian mother-in-law, and raising bilingual daughters. But no one realizes that over the years she has also invested that efficiency in a great many amorous games with the experienced and demanding Roberto. On their honeymoon, in Bangkok, they'd spent one night with two polite teenagers selected from a numbered lineup behind a large glass window. But that was twelve years ago, and although Ariel is not clear about her motives for giving this birthday present, she sees with perfect feminine good sense that she is not meant to be onstage with a pair of young whores who look like angels.

The plan is that Ariel will make a date with Roberto for a dinner in town, and that instead of Ariel, Beba and her colleague will meet him. After dinner the three of them will go to the minuscule apartment near Corso Venezia that Flavio keeps as his sole gesture of independence from his wife. Ariel has insisted on dinner, though Flavio was against it, and Beba has told her, with a tinge of amusement, that it will cost a lot more. Most clients, she says, don't request dinner. Why Ariel should insist that her husband sit around chummily with two hookers, ordering antipasto, first and second courses, and dessert is a mystery, even to Ariel. Yet she feels that it is the proper thing to do. That's the way she wants it, and she can please herself, can't she?

As they finish making the arrangements, Ariel is embarrassed to hear herself say, "I do hope you two girls will make things very nice. My husband is a wonderful man."

And Beba, who is clearly used to talking to wives, assures her, with phenomenal patience, that she understands.

As Ariel puts down the phone, it rings again, and of course it is her mother, calling from the States. "Well, you're finally free," says her mother, who seems to be chewing something, probably a low-calorie bagel, since it is 8:00 A.M. in Bethesda. "Who on earth were you talking to for so long?"

"I was planning Roberto's birthday party," Ariel says glibly. "We're inviting some people to dinner at the golf club."

"Golf! I've never understood how you can live in Italy and be so suburban. Golf in the hills of Giotto!"

"The hills of Giotto are in Umbria, Mom. This is Lombardy, so we're allowed to play golf."

Ariel can envision her mother, unlike Beba, with perfect clarity: tiny; wiry, as if the muscles under her porcelain skin were steel guitar strings. Sitting bolt upright in her condominium kitchen, dressed in the chic, funky uniform of black jeans and cashmere T-shirt she wears to run the business she dreamed up: an improbably successful fleet of suburban messengers on Vespas, which she claims was inspired by her favorite film, *Roman Holiday*. Coffee and soy milk in front of her, quartz-and-silver earrings quivering, one glazed fingernail tapping the counter as her eyes probe the distance over land and ocean toward her only daughter.

What would she say if she knew of the previous call? Almost certainly, Ariel thinks, she would be pleased with an act indicative of the gumption she finds constitutionally lacking in her child, whose lamentable conventionality has been a byword since Ariel was small. She herself is living out a green widowhood with notable style, and dating a much younger lobbyist, whose sexual tastes she would be glad to discuss, girl to girl, with her daughter. But she is loath to shock Ariel.

With her Italian son-in-law, Ariel's mother flirts shamelessly, the established joke being that she should have got there first. It's a joke that never fails to pull a grudging smile from Roberto, and it goes over well with *his* mother, too: another glamorous widow, an intellectual from Padua who regards her daughter-in-law with the condescending solicitude one might reserve for a prize broodmare. For years, Ariel has lived in the dust stirred up by these two dynamos, and it looks as if her daughters, as they grow older – they are eight and ten – are beginning to side with their grandmothers. Not one of these females, it seems, can forgive Ariel for being herself. So Ariel keeps quiet about her new acquaintance with Beba, not from any prudishness but as a powerful amulet. The way, at fourteen, she hugged close the knowledge that she was no longer a virgin.

"Is anything the matter?" asks her mother. "Your voice sounds strange. You and Roberto aren't fighting, are you?" She sighs. "I have told you a hundred times that these spoiled Italian men are naturally promiscuous, so they need a woman who commands interest. You need to be effervescent, on your toes, a little bit slutty, too, if you'll pardon me, darling. Otherwise, they just go elsewhere."

Inspired by her own lie, Ariel actually gives a dinner at the golf club, two days before Roberto's birthday. The clubhouse is a refurbished nineteenth-century castle built by an industrialist, and the terrace where the party is held overlooks the pool and an artificial lake. Three dozen of their friends gather in the late September chill to eat a faux-rustic seasonal feast, consisting of polenta and *Fassone* beefsteaks, and the pungent yellow mushrooms called *funghi reali*, all covered with layers of shaved Alba truffles. Ariel is proud of the meal, planned with the club chef in less time than she spent talking to Beba on the phone.

Roberto is a lawyer, chief counsel for a centrist political party that is moderately honest as Italian political parties go, and his friends all have the same gloss of material success and moderate honesty. Though the group is an international one – many of the men have indulged in American wives as they have in German cars – the humor is typically bourgeois Italian. That is: gossipy, casually cruel, and – in honor of Roberto – all about sex and potency. Somebody passes around an article from *L'Espresso* which celebrates men over fifty with third and fourth wives in their twenties, and everyone glances slyly at Ariel. And Roberto's two oldest friends, Flavio and Michele, appear, bearing a large gift-wrapped box. It turns out to hold not a midget stripper, as someone guesses, but a smaller box, and a third, and a fourth and fifth, until, to cheers, Roberto unwraps a tiny package of Viagra.

Standing over fifty-five smoking candles in a huge pear-and-chocolate torte, he thanks his friends with truculent grace. Everyone laughs and claps – Robert Furioso, as his nickname goes, is famous for his ornery disposition. He doesn't look at Ariel, who is leading the applause in her role as popular second wife and good sport. She doesn't have to look at him to feel his presence, as always, burned into her consciousness. He is a small, charismatic man with a large Greek head, thick, brush-cut black hair turning a uniform steel gray, thin lips hooking downward in an ingrained frown like those of his grandfather, a Sicilian baron. When Ariel met him, a dozen years ago, at the wedding of a distant cousin of hers outside Florence, she immediately recognized the overriding will she had always dreamed of, a force capable of conferring a shape on her own personality. He, prisoner of his desire as surely as she was, looked at this preposterously tall, absurdly placid American beauty as they danced for the third time. And blurted out – a magical phrase that fixed forever the parameters of Ariel's private mythology – "*Tu sai che ti sposerò*. You know I'm going to marry you."

Nowadays Roberto is still *furioso*, but it is at himself for getting old, and at her for witnessing it. So he bullies her, and feels quite justified in doing so. Like all second wives, Ariel was supposed to be a solution, and now she has simply enlarged the problem.

Roberto's birthday begins with blinding sunlight, announcing the brilliant fall weather that arrives when transalpine winds bundle the smog out to sea. The view from Ariel's house on the hill is suddenly endless, as if a curtain had been yanked aside. The steel blue Alps are the first thing she sees through the window at seven-thirty, when her daughters, according to family custom, burst into their parents' bedroom pushing a battered baby carriage with balloons tied to it, and presents inside. Elisa and Cristina, giggling, singing "Happy Birthday," tossing their pretty blunt-cut hair, serene in the knowledge that their irascible father, who loathes sudden awakenings, is putty in their hands. Squeals, kisses, tumbling in the bed, so that Ariel can feel how their cherished small limbs are growing polished, sleeker, more muscular with weekly horseback riding and gymnastics. Bilingual, thanks to their summers in Maryland, they are still more Italian than American; at odd detached moments in her genuinely blissful hours of maternal bustling, Ariel has noticed how, like all other young Italian girls, they exude a precocious maturity. And though they are at times suffocatingly attached to her, there has never been a question about which parent takes precedence. For their father's presents, they have clubbed together to buy from the Body Shop some soap and eye gel and face cream that are made with royal jelly. "To make you look younger, Papa," says Elisa, arriving, as usual, at the painful crux of the matter.

"Are we really going to spend the night at Nonna Silvana's?" Cristina asks Ariel.

"Yes," Ariel replies, feeling a blush rising from under her nightgown. "Yes, because Papa and I are going to dinner in the city."

The girls cheer. They love staying with their Italian grandmother, who stuffs them with marrons glacés and Kit Kat bars and lets them try on all her Pucci outfits from the sixties.

When breakfast – a birthday breakfast, with chocolate brioche – is finished, and the girls are waiting in the car for her to take them to school, Ariel hands Roberto a small gift-wrapped package. He is on the way out the door, his jovial paternal mask back in its secret compartment. "A surprise," she says. "Don't open it before this evening." He looks it over and shakes it suspiciously. "I hope you didn't go and spend money on something else I don't need," he says. "That party—"

"Oh, you'll find a use for this," says Ariel in the seamlessly cheerful voice she has perfected over the years. Inside the package is a million lire in large bills, and the key to Flavio's apartment, as well as a gorgeous pair of silk-and-lace underpants that Ariel has purchased in a size smaller than she usually wears. There is also a note suggesting that Roberto, like a prince in a fairy tale, should search for the best fit in the company in which he finds himself. The note is witty and slightly obscene, the kind of thing Roberto likes. An elegant, wifely touch for a husband who, like all Italian men, is fussy about small things.

Dropping off the girls at the International School, Ariel runs through the usual catechism about when and where they will be picked up, reminders about gym clothes, a note to a geography teacher. She restrains herself from kissing them with febrile intensity, as if she were about to depart on a long journey. Instead she watches as they disappear into a thicket of coltish legs, quilted navy blue jackets, giggles and secrets. She waves to other mothers, Italian, American, Swiss: well-groomed women with tragic morning expressions, looking small inside huge Land Cruisers that could carry them, if necessary, through Lapland or across the Zambezi.

Ariel doesn't want to talk to anyone this morning, but her rambunctious English friend Carinth nabs her and insists on coffee. The two women sit in the small *pasticceria* where all the mothers buy their pastries and chocolates, and Ariel sips barley cappuccino and listens to Carinth go on about her cystitis. Although Ariel is deeply distracted, she is damned if she is going to let anything slip, not even to her loyal friend with the milkmaid's complexion and the lascivious eyes. Damned if she will turn Roberto's birthday into just another easily retailed feminine secret. Avoiding temptation, she looks defiantly around the shop at shelves of meringues, marzipan, candied violets, chocolate chests filled with gilded chocolate cigars, glazed almonds for weddings and first communions, birthday cakes like Palm Beach mansions. The smell of sugar is overpowering. And, for just a second, for the only time all day, her eyes sting with tears.

At home, there are hours to get through. First, she e-mails an article on a Milanese packaging designer to one of the American magazines for which she does freelance translations. Then she telephones to cancel her lesson in the neighboring village with an old artisan who is teaching her to restore antique *papiers peints*, a craft she loves and at which her large hands are surprisingly skillful. Then she goes outside to talk to the garden contractors – three illegal Romanian immigrants who are rebuilding an eroded slope on the east side of the property. She has to haggle with them, and as she does, the leader, an outrageously handsome boy of twenty, looks her over with insolent admiration. Pretty boys don't go unnoticed by Ariel, who sometimes imagines complicated sex with strangers in uncomfortable public places. But they don't really exist for her, just as the men who flirt with her at parties don't count. Only Roberto exists, which is how it has been since that long-ago third dance, when she drew a circle between the two of them and the rest of the world. This is knowledge that she keeps even from Roberto, because she thinks that it would bore him, along with everyone else. Yet is it really so dull to want only one man, the man one already has?

After the gardeners leave, there is nothing to do – no children to pick up at school and ferry to activities; no homework to help with, no dinner to fix. The dogs are at the vet for a wash and a checkup. Unthinkable to invite Carinth or another friend for lunch; unthinkable, too, to return to work, to go shopping, to watch a video or read a book. No, there is nothing but to accept the fact that for an afternoon she has to be the loneliest woman in the world.

Around three o'clock, she gets in the car and heads along the state highway toward Lake Como, where over the years she has taken so many visiting relatives. She has a sudden desire to see the lovely decaying villas sleeping in the trees, the ten-kilometer expanse of lake stretching to the mountains like a predictable future. But as she drives from Greggio to San Giovanni Canavese, past yellowing cornfields, provincial factories, rural discotheques, and ancient village churches, she understands why she is out here. At roadside clearings strewn with refuse, she sees the usual highway prostitutes waiting for afternoon customers.

Ariel has driven past them for years, on her way to her mother-in-law's house or chauffeuring her daughters to riding lessons. Like everyone else, she has first deplored and then come to terms with the fact that the roadside girls are part of a criminal world so successful and accepted that their slavery has routines like those of factory workers: they are transported to and from their ten-hour shifts by a neat fleet of minivans. They are as much a part of the landscape as toll booths.

First, she sees a brown-haired Albanian girl who doesn't look much older than Elisa, wearing black hot pants and a loose white shirt that she lifts like an ungainly wing and flaps slowly at passing drivers. A Fiat Uno cruising in front of Ariel slows down, makes a sudden U-turn, and heads back toward the girl. A kilometer further on are two Nigerians, one dressed in an electric pink playsuit, sitting waggling her knees on an upended crate, while the other, in a pair of stiltlike platform shoes, stands chatting into a cellular phone. Both are tall, with masses of fake braids, and disconcertingly beautiful. Dark seraphim whose presence at the filthy roadside is a kind of miracle.

Ariel slows down to take a better look at the girl in pink, who offers her a noncommittal stare, with eyes opaque as coffee beans. The two-lane road is deserted, and Ariel actually stops the car for a minute, because she feels attracted by those eyes, suddenly mesmerized by something that recalls the secret she heard in Beba's voice. The secret that seemed to be happiness, but, she realizes now, was something different: a mysterious certitude that draws her like a magnet. She feels absurdly moved – out of control, in fact. As her heart pounds, she realizes that if she let herself go, she would open the door and crawl toward that flat dark gaze. The girl in pink says something to her companion with the phone, who swivels on the three-inch soles of her shoes to look at

Ariel. And Ariel puts her foot on the gas pedal. Ten kilometers down the road, she stops again and yanks out a Kleenex to wipe the film of sweat from her face. The only observation she allows herself as she drives home, recovering her composure, is the thought of how curious it is that all of them are foreigners – herself, Beba, and the girls on the road.

Six o'clock. As she walks into the house, the phone rings, and it is Flavio, who asks how the plot is progressing. Ariel can't conceal her impatience.

"Listen, do you think those girls are going to be on time?"

"As far as I know, they are always punctual," he says. "But I have to go. I'm calling from the car here in the garage, and it's starting to look suspicious."

He hangs up, but Ariel stands with the receiver in her hand, struck by the fact that besides worrying about whether dinner guests, upholsterers, baby-sitters, restorers of wrought iron, and electricians will arrive on schedule, she now has to concern herself with whether Beba will keep her husband waiting.

Seven-thirty. The thing now is not to answer the phone. If he thinks of her, which is unlikely, Roberto must assume that she is in the car, dressed in one of the discreetly sexy short black suits or dresses she wears for special occasions, her feet in spike heels pressing the accelerator as she speeds diligently to their eight o'clock appointment. He is still in the office, firing off the last frantic fax to Rome, pausing for a bit of ritual abuse aimed at his harassed assistant, Amedeo. Next, he will dash for a pee in his grim brown-marble bathroom: how well she can envision the last, impatient shake of his cock, which is up for an unexpected adventure tonight. He will grab a handful of the chocolates that the doctor has forbidden, and gulp down a paper cup of sugary espresso from the office machine. Then into the shiny late-model Mercedes – a monument, he calls it, with an unusual flash of self-mockery, to the male climacteric. After which, becalmed in the Milan evening traffic, he may call her. Just to make sure she is going to be on time.

Eight-fifteen. She sits at the kitchen table and eats a frugal meal: a plate of rice with cheese and olive oil, a sliced tomato, a glass of water.

The phone rings again. She hesitates, then picks it up.

It is Roberto. *"Allora, sei rimasta a casa,"* he says softly. "So you stayed home."

"Yes, of course," she replies, keeping her tone light. "It's your birthday, not mine. How do you like your present? Are they gorgeous?"

He laughs, and she feels weak with relief. "They're impressive. They're not exactly dressed for a restaurant, though. Why on earth did you think I needed to eat dinner with them? I keep hoping I won't run into anybody I know."

In the background, she hears the muted roar of an eating house, the uniform evening hubbub of voices, glasses, silver, plates.

"Where are you calling from?" Ariel asks.

"Beside the cashier's desk. I have to go. I can't be rude. I'll call you later."

"Good luck," she says. She is shocked to find a streak of malice in her tone, and still more shocked at the sense of power she feels as she puts down the phone. Leaving him trapped in a restaurant, forced to make conversation with two whores, while the other diners stare and the waiters shoot him roguish grins. Was that panic she heard in Roberto's voice? And what could that naughty Beba and her friend be wearing? Not cheap hot pants like the road-side girls, she hopes. For the price, one would expect at least Versace.

After that, there is nothing for Ariel to do but kick off her shoes and wander through her house, her bare feet unexpectedly warm on the waxed surface of the old terra-cotta tiles she spent months collecting from junkyards and wrecked villas. She locks the doors and puts on the alarm, but turns on only the hall and stairway lights. And then walks like a night watchman from room to darkened room, feeling flashes of uxorious pride at the sight of furnishings she knows as well as her own body. *Uxorious* – the incongruous word actually floats through her head as her glance passes over the flourishes of a Piedmontese Baroque cabinet in the dining room, a watchful congregation of Barbies in the girls' playroom, a chubby Athena in a Mantuan painting in the upstairs hall. When has Ariel ever moved through the house in such freedom? It is exhilarating, and slightly appalling. And she receives the strange impression that this is the real reason she has staged this birthday stunt: to be alone and in conscious possession of the solitude she has accumulated over the years. To contemplate, for as long as she likes, the darkness in her own house. At the top of the stairs she stops for a minute and then slowly begins to take off her clothes, letting them fall softly at her feet. Then, naked, she sits down on the top step, the cold stone numbing her bare backside. Her earlier loneliness has evaporated: the shadows she is studying seem to be friendly presences jostling to keep her company. She relaxes back on her elbows, and playfully bobs her knees, like the roadside girl on the crate.

Ten o'clock. Bedtime. What she has wanted it to be since this afternoon. A couple of melatonin, a glass of dark Danish stout whose bitter concentrated taste of hops makes her sleepy. A careful shower, cleaning of teeth, application of face and body creams, a gray cotton nightdress. She could, she thinks, compose a specialized etiquette guide for women in her situation. One's goal is to exude an air of extreme cleanliness and artless beauty. One washes and dries one's hair, but does not apply perfume or put on any garment that could be construed as seductive. The subtle enchantment to be cast is that of a homespun Elysium, the appeal of Penelope after Calypso.

By ten-thirty, she is sitting up in bed with the *Herald Tribune*, reading a history of the FBI's Most Wanted list. Every few seconds, she attempts quite coolly to think of what Roberto is inevitably doing by now, but she determines that it is actually impossible to do so. Those two pages in her imagination are stuck together.

She does, however, recall the evening in Bangkok that she and Roberto spent with the pair of massage girls. How the four of them walked in silence to a fluorescent-lit room with a huge plastic bathtub, and how the two terrifyingly polite, terrifyingly young girls, slick with soapsuds, massaging her with their small plump breasts and shaven pubes, reminded her of nothing so much as chickens washed and trussed for the oven. And how the whole event threatened to become a theater of disaster, until Ariel saw that she would have to manage things. How she indicated to the girls by a number of discreet signs that the three of them were together in acting out a private performance for the man in the room. How the girls understood and even seemed relieved, and how much pleasure her husband took in what, under her covert direction, they all contrived. How she felt less like an erotic performer than a social director setting out to save an awkward party. And how silent she was afterward – not the silence of shocked schoolgirl sensibilities, as Roberto, no doubt, assumed, but the silence of amazement at a world where she always had to be a hostess.

She turns out the light and dreams that she is flying with other people in a plane precariously tacked together from wooden crates and old car parts. They land in the Andes, and she sees that all the others are women and that they are naked, as she is. They are all sizes and colors, and she is far from being the prettiest, but is not the ugliest, either. They are there to film an educational television special, BBC or PBS, and the script says to improvise a dance, which they all do earnestly and clumsily: Scottish reels, belly dancing, and then Ariel suggests ring-around-the-rosy, which turns out to be more fun than anyone had bargained for, as they all flop down, giggling at the end. The odd thing about this dream is how completely happy it is.

She wakes to noise in the room, and Roberto climbing into bed and embracing her. "Dutiful," she thinks, as he kisses her and reaches for her breasts, but then she lets the thought go. He smells alarmingly clean, but it is a soap she knows. As they make love, he offers her a series of verbal sketches from the evening he has just passed, a bit like a child listing his new toys. What he says is not exciting, but it is exciting to hear him trying, for her benefit, to sound scornful and detached. And the familiar geography of his body has acquired a passing air of mystery, simply because she knows that other women – no matter how resolutely transient and hasty – have been examining it. For the first time in as long as she can remember, she is curious about Roberto.

"Were they really so beautiful?" she asks, when, lying in the dark, they resume coherent conversation. "Flavio said that seeing them was like entering paradise."

Roberto gives an arrogant, joyful laugh that sounds as young as a teenage boy's.

"Only for an old idiot like Flavio. They were flashy, let's put it that way. The dark one, Beba, had an amazing body, but her friend had a better face. The worst thing was having to eat with them – and in that horrendous restaurant. Whose idea was that, yours or Flavio's?" His voice grows comically aggrieved. "It was the kind of tourist place where they wheel a cart of mints and chewing gum to your table after the coffee. And those girls asked for doggie bags, can you imagine? They filled them with Chiclets!"

The two of them are lying in each other's arms, shaking with laughter as they haven't done for months, even years. And Ariel is swept for an instant by a heady sense of accomplishment. "Which of them won the underpants?" she asks.

"What? Oh, I didn't give them away. They were handmade, silk, expensive stuff – too nice for a hooker. I kept them for you."

"But they're too small for me," protests Ariel.

"Well, exchange them. You did save the receipt, I hope." Roberto's voice, which has been affectionate, indulgent, as in their best times together, takes on a shade of its normal domineering impatience. But it is clear that he is still abundantly pleased, both with himself and with her. Yawning, he announces that he has to get some sleep, that he's out of training for this kind of marathon. That he didn't even fortify himself with his birthday Viagra. He alludes to an old private joke of theirs by remarking that Ariel's present proves conclusively that his mother was right in warning him against immoral American women; and he gives her a final kiss. Adding a possessive, an uxorious, squeeze of her bottom. Then he settles down and lies so still that she thinks he is already asleep. Until, out of a long silence, he whispers, "Thank you."

In a few minutes he is snorting. But Ariel lies still and relaxed, with her arms at her sides and her eyes wide open. She has always rationed her illusions, and has been married too long to be shocked by the swiftness with which her carefully perverse entertainment has dissolved into the fathomless triviality of domestic life. In a certain way that swiftness is Ariel's triumph – a measure of the strength of the quite ordinary bondage that, years ago, she chose for herself. So it doesn't displease her to know that she will wake up tomorrow, make plans to retrieve her daughters, and find that nothing has changed.

But no, she thinks, turning on her side, something is different. A sense of loss is creeping over her, and she realizes it is because she misses Beba. Beba who for two weeks has lent a penumbral glamour to Ariel's days. Beba, who, in the best of fantasies, might have sent a comradely message home to her through Roberto. But, of course, there is no message, and it is clear that the party is over. The angels have flown, leaving Ariel – good wife and faithful spirit – awake in the dark with considerable consolations: a sleeping man, a silent house, and the knowledge that, with her usual practicality, she has kept Beba's number.

Raymond Carver
(Born in Oregon; 1938–88)

"The Bath" is a short version of Carver's "A Small, Good Thing". In fact, it was the result of much reworking by a powerful "minimalist" editor; Carver himself, less than pleased with it, later produced the longer version. "A Small, Good Thing" is certainly the superior work with its deeper content but "The Bath" has its own special flavour. The truly bleak impression it leaves, as if it has had its head lopped off for no reason, is not to be found elsewhere.

The overwhelming majority of Carver's early works deal with loss and despair, but later an element of redemption enters in, bringing depth and breadth and warmth to his world. Comparing "The Bath" with "A Small, Good Thing," the reader has a vivid demonstration of the drastic change.

The Bath

BY RAYMOND CARVER

Saturday afternoon the mother drove to the bakery in the shopping center. After looking through a loose-leaf binder with photographs of cakes taped onto the pages, she ordered chocolate, the child's favorite. The cake she chose was decorated with a spaceship and a launching pad under a sprinkling of white stars. The name SCOTTY would be iced on in green as if it were the name of the spaceship.

The baker listened thoughtfully when the mother told him Scotty would be eight years old. He was an older man, this baker, and he wore a curious apron, a heavy thing with loops that went under his arms and around his back and then crossed in front again where they were tied in a very thick knot. He kept wiping his hands on the front of the apron as he listened to the woman, his wet eyes examining her lips as she studied the samples and talked.

He let her take her time. He was in no hurry.

The mother decided on the spaceship cake, and then she gave the baker her name and her telephone number. The cake would be ready Monday morning, in plenty of time for the party Monday afternoon. This was all the baker was willing to say. No pleasantries, just this small exchange, the barest information, nothing that was not necessary.

Monday morning, the boy was walking to school. He was in the company of another boy, the two boys passing a bag of potato chips back and forth between them. The birthday boy was trying to trick the other boy into telling what he was going to give in the way of a present.

At an intersection, without looking, the birthday boy stepped off the curb, and was promptly knocked down by a car. He fell on his side, his head in the gutter, his legs in the road moving as if he were climbing a wall.

The other boy stood holding the potato chips. He was wondering if he should finish the rest or continue on to school.

The birthday boy did not cry. But neither did he wish to talk anymore. He would not answer when the other boy asked what it felt like to be hit by a car. The birthday boy got up and turned back for home, at which time the other boy waved good-bye and headed off for school.

The birthday boy told his mother what had happened. They sat together on the sofa. She held his hands in her lap. This is what she was doing when the boy pulled his hands away and lay down on his back.

Of course, the birthday party never happened. The birthday boy was in the hospital instead. The mother sat by the bed. She was waiting for the boy to wake up. The father hurried over from his office. He sat next to the mother. So now the both of them waited for the boy to wake up. They waited for hours, and then the father went home to take a bath.

The man drove home from the hospital. He drove the streets faster than he should. It had been a good life till now. There had been work, fatherhood, family. The man had been lucky and happy. But fear made him want a bath.

He pulled into the driveway. He sat in the car trying to make his legs work. The child had been hit by a car and he was in the hospital, but he was going to be all right. The man got out of the car and went up to the door. The dog was barking and the telephone was ringing. It kept ringing while the man unlocked the door and felt the wall for the light switch.

He picked up the receiver. He said, "I just got in the door!"

"There's a cake that wasn't picked up."

This is what the voice on the other end said.

"What are you saying?" the father said.

"The cake," the voice said. "Sixteen dollars."

The husband held the receiver against his ear, trying to understand. He said, "I don't know anything about it."

"Don't hand me that," the voice said.

The husband hung up the telephone. He went into the kitchen and poured himself some whiskey. He called the hospital.

The child's condition remained the same.

While the water ran into the tub, the man lathered his face and shaved. He was in the tub when he heard the telephone again. He got himself out and hurried through the house, saying, "Stupid, stupid," because he wouldn't be doing this if he'd stayed where he was in the hospital. He picked up the receiver and shouted, "Hello!"

The voice said, "It's ready."

The father got back to the hospital after midnight. The wife was sitting in the chair by the bed. She looked up at the husband and then she looked back at the child. From an apparatus over the bed hung a bottle with a tube running from the bottle to the child.

"What's this?" the father said.

"Glucose," the mother said.

The husband put his hand to the back of the woman's head.

"He's going to wake up," the man said.

"I know," the woman said.

In a little while the man said, "Go home and let me take over."

She shook her head. "No," she said.

"Really," he said. "Go home for a while. You don't have to worry. He's sleeping, is all."

A nurse pushed open the door. She nodded to them as she went to the bed. She took the left arm out from under the covers and put her fingers on the wrist. She put the arm back under the covers and wrote on the clipboard attached to the bed.

"How is he?" the mother said.

"Stable," the nurse said. Then she said, "Doctor will be in again shortly."

"I was saying maybe she'd want to go home and get a little rest," the man said. "After the doctor comes."

"She could do that," the nurse said.

The woman said, "We'll see what the doctor says." She brought her hand up to her eyes and leaned her head forward.

The nurse said, "Of course."

The father gazed at his son, the small chest inflating and deflating under the covers. He felt more fear now. He began shaking his head. He talked to himself like this. The child is fine. Instead of sleeping at home, he's doing it here. Sleep is the same wherever you do it.

The doctor came in. He shook hands with the man. The woman got up from the chair.

"Ann," the doctor said and nodded. The doctor said, "Let's just see how he's doing." He moved to the bed and touched the boy's wrist. He peeled back an eyelid and then the other. He turned back the covers and listened to the heart. He pressed his fingers here and there on the body. He went to the end of the bed and studied the chart. He noted the time, scribbled on the chart, and then he considered the mother and the father.

This doctor was a handsome man. His skin was moist and tan. He wore a three-piece suit, a vivid tie, and on his shirt were cufflinks.

The mother was talking to herself like this. He has just come from somewhere with an audience. They gave him a special medal.

The doctor said, "Nothing to shout about, but nothing to worry about. He should wake up pretty soon." The doctor looked at the boy again. "We'll know more after the tests are in."

"Oh, no," the mother said.

The doctor said, "Sometimes you see this."

The father said, "You wouldn't call this a coma, then?" The father waited and looked at the doctor.

"No, I don't want to call it that," the doctor said. "He's sleeping. It's restorative. The body is doing what it has to do."

"It's a coma," the mother said. "A kind of coma."

The doctor said, "I wouldn't call it that."

He took the woman's hands and patted them. He shook hands with the husband.

The woman put her fingers on the child's forehead and kept them there for a while. "At least he doesn't have a fever," she said. Then she said, "I don't know. Feel his head."

The man put his fingers on the boy's forehead. The man said, "I think he's supposed to feel this way."

The woman stood there awhile longer, working her lip with her teeth. Then she moved to her chair and sat down.

The husband sat in the chair beside her. He wanted to say something else. But there was no saying what it should be. He took her hand and put it in his lap. This made him feel better. It made him feel he was saying something. They sat like that for a while, watching the boy, not talking. From time to time he squeezed her hand until she took it away.

"I've been praying," she said.

"Me too," the father said. "I've been praying too."

A nurse came back in and checked the flow from the bottle.

A doctor came in and said what his name was. This doctor was wearing loafers.

"We're going to take him downstairs for more pictures," he said. "And we want to do a scan."

"A scan?" the mother said. She stood between this new doctor and the bed.

"It's nothing," he said.

"My God," she said.

Two orderlies came in. They wheeled a thing like a bed. They unhooked the boy from the tube and slid him over onto the thing with wheels.

It was after sunup when they brought the birthday boy back out. The mother and father followed the orderlies into the elevator and up to the room. Once more the parents took up their places next to the bed.

They waited all day. The boy did not wake up. The doctor came again and examined the boy again and left after saying the same things again. Nurses came in. Doctors came in. A technician came in and took blood.

"I don't understand this," the mother said to the technician.

"Doctor's orders," the technician said.

The mother went to the window and looked out at the parking lot. Cars with their lights on were driving in and out. She stood at the window with her hands on the sill. She was talking to herself like this. We're into something now, something hard.

She was afraid.

She saw a car stop and a woman in a long coat get into it. She made believe she was that woman. She made believe she was driving away from here to someplace else.

The doctor came in. He looked tanned and healthier than ever. He went to the bed and examined the boy. He said, "His signs are fine. Everything's good."

The mother said, "But he's sleeping."

"Yes," the doctor said.

The husband said, "She's tired. She's starved."

The doctor said, "She should rest. She should eat. Ann," the doctor said.

"Thank you," the husband said.

He shook hands with the doctor and the doctor patted their shoulders and left.

"I suppose one of us should go home and check on things," the man said. "The dog needs to be fed."

"Call the neighbors," the wife said. "Someone will feed him if you ask them to."

She tried to think who. She closed her eyes and tried to think anything at all. After a time she said, "Maybe I'll do it. Maybe if I'm not here watching, he'll wake up. Maybe it's because I'm watching that he won't."

"That could be it," the husband said.

"I'll go home and take a bath and put on something clean," the woman said.

"I think you should do that," the man said.

She picked up her purse. He helped her into her coat. She moved to the door, and looked back. She looked at the child, and then she looked at the father. The husband nodded and smiled.

She went past the nurses' station and down to the end of the corridor, where she turned and saw a little waiting room, a family in there, all sitting in wicker chairs, a man in a khaki shirt, a baseball cap pushed back on his head, a large woman wearing a housedress, slippers, a girl in jeans, hair in dozens of kinky braids, the table littered with flimsy wrappers and styrofoam and coffee sticks and packets of salt and pepper.

"Nelson," the woman said. "Is it about Nelson?"

The woman's eyes widened.

"Tell me now, lady," the woman said. "Is it about Nelson?"

The woman was trying to get up from her chair. But the man had his hand closed over her arm.

"Here, here," the man said.

"I'm sorry," the mother said. "I'm looking for the elevator. My son is in the hospital. I can't find the elevator."

"Elevator is down that way," the man said, and he aimed a finger in the right direction.

"My son was hit by a car," the mother said. "But he's going to be all right. He's in shock now, but it might be some kind of coma too. That's what worries us, the coma part. I'm going out for a while. Maybe I'll take a bath. But my husband is with him. He's watching. There's a chance everything will change when I'm gone. My name is Ann Weiss."

The man shifted in his chair. He shook his head.

He said, "Our Nelson."

She pulled into the driveway. The dog ran out from behind the house. He ran in circles on the grass. She closed her eyes and leaned her head against the wheel. She listened to the ticking of the engine.

She got out of the car and went to the door. She turned on lights and put on water for tea. She opened a can and fed the dog. She sat down on the sofa with her tea.

The telephone rang.

"Yes!" she said. "Hello!" she said.

"Mrs. Weiss," a man's voice said.

"Yes," she said. "This is Mrs. Weiss. Is it about Scotty?" she said.

"Scotty," the voice said. "It is about Scotty," the voice said. "It has to do with Scotty, yes."

Paul Theroux
(Born in Massachusetts, 1941)

This is an excerpt from Theroux's 2001 novel *Hotel Honolulu*. Structured more like an assemblage of short stories the novel has chapters that can be read independently of one another. The central character of the book is a once-famous travel writer who has decided to settle down in Honolulu as the manager of a second-rate hotel. The reader may well see him as an image of Theroux himself (Theroux has in fact spent half his life in Hawaii).

Theroux first made a name for himself as a travel writer, but many readers were drawn to the fresh point of view of those early works of his for their ability to discover a special brand of humour in virtually everything. The theme of his fiction might be boiled down to something like this: he tells stories of people who go on searching for paradise and who are betrayed in the process. *Hotel Honolulu* is a novel that can be read for the sheer fun of it.

A Game of Dice

BY PAUL THEROUX

Leaving our Paradise Lost bar, shouldering his way through the hotel lobby, the young man caught my eye and said, "Now I've heard everything!" in a provocative way, too loudly, to get my attention. I was hoping my silence and my bland smile would calm him.

"Can I help you?" I said. "I'm the manager."

In his early thirties and handsome – all that springy hair – he wore a dark shirt that set off his pink impatient face. Breathless and a bit flustered, he looked like someone who had just been disarmed by an insult. The way a man looks when he's slapped by a woman.

"See that guy? He's out of his mind!"

He was gone before I could tell him that the man he had pointed out, Eddie Alfanta, was a regular at the bar, always came with his wife, Cheryl, whom he adored, and was a well-known accountant downtown – overserious but successful, with an office on Bishop Street. What I liked most about him was his passion for gambling. Eddie was not the first accountant I had known who gambled, though the risks of the crap table and the solemnity of the ledger made him seem paradoxical and confident. His wagers were modest. He usually won. He said he had a system.

So intent was Eddie on peering around the bar that he did not see me. Where was his wife? Cheryl was a small woman, elfin almost – short hair, delicate bones, tiny hands and feet, very tidy, always neatly dressed, and pale, especially in contrast to big, dark Eddie Alfanta, who boasted of his hairiness. That Eddie was also proud of Cheryl, his *haole* trophy, was plain to see, and he had the slightly fussy henpecked demeanor that characterized the ethnic partner in many Hawaiian interracial marriages. He was self-conscious, eager to do the right thing but not sure what the right thing was, and had the uneasy notion that people were watching. And they were.

The next time I checked the bar, I saw Eddie with the dice cup in his hand, shaking it, making it chuckle. Buddy Hamstra had brought the leather cup and the pair of dice from Bangkok, where men in bars tossed dice to determine who would pay for the next round of drinks. I often studied the fixed attentive faces and bared teeth of the men going at it and thought how we are at our most aggressive and competitive, most animalistic, in our games.

What I noticed tonight was not the game but Eddie's opponent. We seldom saw surfers in Paradise Lost. The better class of surfer, one of Trey's buddies, out for a week of catching waves, yes, but never a local full-season hard-core dude like this one – barefoot, broad-shouldered, bandy-legged, tattoos on the small of his back and another between his shoulder blades, with the name CODY, all the tattoos visible through his torn shirt. His cap on backward, his long hair was sunned, the color and texture of straw, his eyes pale and vacant, his skin burned, his masses of freckles, big and small, adding to his look of recklessness. He was young, probably not more than twenty-two or -three. Eddie Alfanta was over forty, so it looked funny, the two of them struggling with the dice cup: the swarthy accountant with his shirt tucked in and two pens in his breast pocket, the youth in ragged shirt and shorts – Stüssy cap, Quiksilver shorts, Local Motion shirt. He had dirty feet, bruised toes.

"A water rat," Trey said.

The two men hovered over the tumbled dice on the bar, and I also thought how sad games are for their rules and rituals, for making us absurdly hopeful, for being pre-dictable, for their pathetic purpose, which was to divert us for the length of time it took to play them. All players looked to me like desperate losers; games were the pas-times of people – always men – who could not bear to be alone, who did not read. There was a brutal pathos in the game of dice, the little chuckle, the toss, the click, the overwhelming significance of the dots.

Or was it just harmless fun that defied interpretation? There was something wrong in my caring about it, or even noticing it, so I turned away and concentrated on what was much more obvious: for the first time Eddie's wife was not with him in the bar. His laughter made that emphatic, and he crowded the surfer, maneuvering the dice cup, making the dice chatter, his mouth open a bit too wide, his laugh-ter a bit too shrill, touching the surfer's arm when he won. Eddie was dark and baked, the boy fair and burned – I sensed attraction. But I was glad they were laughing there; I liked thinking of my hotel as a refuge.

Back at the desk, fishing for information, I mentioned to Chen that Eddie Alfanta was alone in the bar.

"His wife's upstairs," Chen said. "I gave them 802. They checked in a few hours ago. One night."

That was unusual, the Honolulu couple staying in a Honolulu hotel for one night. Maybe it meant that their house was being tented and fumigated, but if so, they would have had the work done on a weekend or else spent the time on a neighbor island.

"These flowers just came for Mrs. Alfanta."

The bouquet was on the desktop. The greeting card read, *Happy birthday, my darling. All my love, Eddie.*

A romantic birthday interlude – it explained everything. I went through the month's occupancy record in my office, and afterward, in search of a drink, I saw Eddie alone in the bar, nursing a beer, looking reflective. There was no sign of the surfer, and I remembered what the fleeing man had said about Eddie earlier in the evening: He's out of his mind.

But Eddie was the picture of serenity. Somewhat quieter than usual, perhaps; alone but content. Had the gambling made him thoughtful? Anyway, the game was at an end.

Had he been rebuffed by the water rat? The last time I had seen him, he was pushing against the young man as the dice clattered onto the bar, shouting for drinks, tapping the young man's tattooed arm. I resisted drawing any conclusions, but it had certainly seemed to me a playful courtship, the two men jostling at the rail in a rough mating dance, laughing over the game of dice.

I said, "Who's winning?" because Eddie was still absentmindedly shaking the cup.

"We're spending the night," he said, and his chuckle was like the sound of the dice.

"So I see," I said, and to test him, because I already knew, I asked, "A celebration?"

"Cheryl's birthday." He tossed the dice, frowned at the combination, and gathered them quickly. "This is a big one. Her fortieth. Last year we went to Vegas. Cheryl's lucky. She won five hundred dollars at the crap table. Guy came up to her and humped her for luck. 'You're on a roll,' they said. You should have seen it."

He stopped and saw the half-smile of concentration on my face. I was thinking, Humped her for luck? He understood the unspoken question in my mind.

"I loved it," he said.

Small, pale Cheryl in her tiny shoes surrounded by big, hopeful gamblers, and Eddie gloating like the winner in a dog show.

"Birthday before that, we spent the weekend learning to scuba-dive. Getting certified. I was terrible. I figured it was a gamble. I almost panicked and drowned. The guys on the course were amazed that Cheryl had picked it up so quickly. They were all over her. You should have seen her – what a knockout in a wetsuit. Skintight."

Pleased with the recollection, he touched his thighs as though tracing a wetsuit, and he gathered the dice again. Another chuckle and toss.

"For her thirty-fifth we had a real blast. My buddy and I took her to Disneyland. She was like a kid." He smiled, remembering, and wheezed with satisfaction. "She wore him out!"

Wagging the dice cup, he rolled again.

"Where is she now?"

"I got her a surfer. They're upstairs." He looked happy. He was still rolling the dice.

"Who won?"

"Who do you think?"

The young man in the torn shirt entering the room, his bruised toes on the carpet, the lamp low, Cheryl in her birthday lingerie, no bigger than a tall child but game for this, and the whole business more or less wordless – this was how I imagined it. The pair of them tossing on the bed with Eddie downstairs. And at the end of it all a certain apprehension, because no one knew what would happen when it was over. That was the sadness of games.

"I have no idea," I said.

Eddie just smiled. He had forgotten the question.

I sent Keola and Kawika up to monitor the corridor near the Alfantas' room in case of trouble. Later, they told me how they had seen the surfer leaving, "Looking fut-less," and heard Cheryl sternly saying, "Don't kiss me." Still later, I saw Cheryl and Eddie very lovey-dovey in the lounge, Eddie still tossing the dice. Perhaps he was the only one who had gotten what he wanted.

Claire Keegan
(Born in Ireland, 1968)

Ms. Keegan belongs to the youngest generation of writers represented in this book. Born in County Wicklow, Ireland, she went to the USA at the age of 17 and spent six years studying English literature and political science at college in New Orleans. She began writing in 1994, publishing the collection from which the present work is taken, *Antarctica*, in 1998. She is now at work on her second book of stories and also a novel.

Keegan uses simple words to write simple sentences that join together to spin out simple (yet warm and deep) scenes. She shows us the world through the eyes of a vulnerable 19-year-old who possesses not even a name. Neither does he attempt to give us his thoughts and feelings directly. Instead, he lets the surrounding scene tell us about himself. He emerges gradually from his world until he stands revealed before us, and then is absorbed back into it again.

Close to the Water's Edge

BY CLAIRE KEEGAN

Tonight he is out on the balcony, his dark tan stunning against the white of his dress shirt. Many days have passed since he left Cambridge, Massachusetts, to spend time at his mother's penthouse on the coast. He does not care for these rooms, with vicious swordfish mounted on the walls and all these mirrors that make it impossible to do even the simplest thing without seeing his reflection.

He stays out on the beach and through his shades watches the bathers, the procession of young men with washboard bellies walking the strand. Women turn over on their deck chairs browning themselves evenly on all sides. They come here with their summer books and sunhats, reaching into their coolers for beer and Coppertone. In the afternoons when the heat becomes unbearable, he swims out to the sandbar, a good half mile from the shore. He can see it now, the strip of angry waves breaking in the shallows. Now the tide is advancing, erasing the white, well-trodden sands. A brown pelican, a small piece of the past, floats by on the Texas wind. Joggers stay close to the water's edge, their shadows fastened like guardians at their sides.

Inside, his mother is arguing with his stepfather, the millionaire who owns these condominiums. After his parents divorced, his mother said that people have no control over who they fall in love with, and soon afterward married the millionaire. Now he can hear them talking, their enraged whispers gathering speed on the slope of their argument. It is an old story.

"I'm warning you, Richard, don't bring it up!"

"Who brought it up? Who?"

"It's his birthday, for Christ's sake!"

"Who said anything?"

The young man looks down. At the hot tub, a mother braces herself and enters the steamy waters. Screams from racing children pierce the air. He feels the same trepidation he always feels at these family occasions, and wonders why he came back here when he could be in Cambridge in his T-shirt and shorts, drinking his Australian beer, playing chess on the computer. He takes the cufflinks from his pocket, a gift his grandmother gave him shortly before she died. They are gold-plated cufflinks whose gold is slowly wearing off, revealing the steel underneath.

When his grandmother first married, she begged her husband to take her to the ocean. They were country people, pig farmers from Tennessee. His grandmother said she had never laid eyes on the Atlantic. She said if she saw the ocean, she could settle down. It wasn't anything she could explain. But each time she asked her husband, his response was the same.

"Who'll feed the pigs?"

"We could ask the neighbors—"

"You can't trust anybody. That's our livelihood out there."

Months passed; she grew heavy with child and finally gave up asking to see the ocean. Then one Sunday her husband shook her awake.

"Pack a bag, Marcie," he said, "we're going to the coast."

It wasn't yet light when they got into the car. They drove all that day, across the hills of Tennessee toward Florida. The landscape changed from green, hilly farmland to dry acres with tall palms and pampas grass. The sun was going down when they arrived. She got out and gasped at the Atlantic, whose end she could not see. It looked green in the evening sun. It wasn't what she expected. It seemed a lonely, infertile place to her, with the stink of seaweed and the gulls fighting for leftovers in the sand.

Then her husband took out his pocket watch.

"One hour, Marcie. I'll give you one hour," he said. "If you're not back by then, you can find your own way home."

She walked for half an hour with her bare feet in the frothy edge of the sea, then turned back along the cliff path, and from the shelter of some trees, watched her husband, at five minutes past the appointed hour, slam the car door and turn the ignition. Just as he was gathering speed, she jumped into the road and stopped the car.

Then she climbed in and spent the rest of her life with a man who would have gone home without her.

His nineteenth birthday is marked by a dinner at Leonardo's, the fancy seafood restaurant overlooking the bay. His mother, dressed in a white pants suit with a rhinestone belt, joins him on the balcony.

"I'm so proud of you, honey."

"Mom," he says and embraces her. She's a small woman with a hot temper. She gazes out at the water.

"Will you fix my tie?" he asks. "I never could do this right."

She knots the silk into an unnecessarily tight bow.

"There," she says. "You'll be the belle of the ball. How many mothers can say, 'My boy's going to Harvard University?' I'm a pig farmer's daughter from Tennessee, and my boy is going to Harvard. When I'm low, I always remember that, and it cheers me up no end."

"Mom!"

"You play your cards right and this could all be yours someday," she says. "He's got no kids. You wonder why I married him, but I was thinking of you all along."

Just then the millionaire comes out with a lighted cigar and blows a mouthful of smoke into the night. He's an ordinary-looking man with the whitest teeth money can buy.

"You-all ready? I could eat a small child," he says.

The restaurant owner greets the millionaire, escorts them to the table. A wooden board of crab claws is brought out. The millionaire eats them with his bare hands and clicks his fingers for the waiter, who pops a champagne cork. He always drinks champagne.

"Did you hear about this guy Clinton? Says if he's

elected president, he's gonna let queers into the military," he says. "What do you think of that, Harvard?"

"Richard," his mother says.

"It's okay, Mom. Well, I don't think—"

"What's next? Lesbians coaching the swim team, running for the Senate?"

"Richard!"

"What kind of defense would that be? A bunch of queers! We didn't win two world wars that way. I don't know what this country is turning into."

Smells of horseradish and dill spill out from the kitchen. A lobster has got loose in the tank, but the waiter dips a net into the water and traps him.

"No more politics," his mother says. "It's my boy's night. He got a 3.75 grade point average last semester. Now what do you think of that, Richard?"

"3.75? Not bad."

"Not bad? Well, I should say not! He's top of his class at Harvard!"

"Mom."

"No, I won't be hushed up this time! He's top of the class, and he's nineteen years old today! A grown man, almost. Let's have a toast."

"Now, there's an idea," says the millionaire. He refills the champagne flutes. "Here's to the brightest young man in the whole state of Florida," he says. (They are smiling now, suddenly at ease. There is a chance that this dinner will not be like the others.) ". . . and to not having queers in the military!"

The mother's smile capsizes. "Goddamn, Richard!"

"What's the matter? It's just a little joke. Doesn't anybody around here know how to take a joke anymore?"

The waiter arrives with a steel tray and the entrées. Turbot for the lady, salmon for the young man, and lobster for the millionaire. The millionaire wants more champagne.

"There must be some fine women up there at Harvard," he says. "Some real knockouts."

"They accept us on the basis of intelligence, not looks."

"Even so. The best and the brightest. How come you never bring a girl down?" The millionaire ties a napkin around his neck, takes the pincers and breaks a claw open, picks out the meat. "They must be all around you like flies," he says, "a young man like you. Why, when I was your age I had a different woman every weekend."

"These olives!" the mother says. "Taste these olives!"

They eat in silence for the rest of the meal, as the millionaire likes to concentrate on his food. Afterward, the maitre d' comes by and whispers a few words into the millionaire's ear. The lights around their table are doused, and a lighted cake is carried from the kitchen by a nervous, Mexican waiter singing "Happy Birthday". It is a pink cake, the pinkest cake the young man has ever seen, like a cake you'd have at a christening party for twin girls. The millionaire is grinning.

"Make a wish, honey!" his mother says.

The young man closes his eyes and makes a wish, then blows hard, extinguishing the candles. The millionaire takes the knife and carves it into uneven pieces, like a pie chart. The young man stuffs a piece into his mouth, licks the frosting. The millionaire reaches for his mother's hand, clasps her jeweled fingers.

"Happy birthday, son," the mother says and kisses him on the mouth. He tastes lipstick, stands, and he hears himself thanking them for a pleasant birthday. He hears his mother calling his name, the waiter saying, "Good evening, sir," at the doorway. He is crossing the highway now, finding a space between the speeding cars. Other college kids are drinking beer on the promenade, watching the bungee jumpers throwing themselves into midair, screaming.

Down at the deserted beach, the tide has reclaimed the strand. The water is rough in the night wind. He loosens the knot at his throat and walks on and on, losing track of time. Up at the pier, yachts with roped-in sails stand trembling on the water. He thinks of his grandmother coming to the ocean. She said if she had her life to live again, she would never have climbed back into that car. She'd have stayed behind and turned into a streetwalker sooner than go home. Nine children she bore him. When her grandson asked what made her get back in, her answer was, "Those were the times I lived in. That's what I believed. I thought I didn't have a choice."

His grandmother, with whom he lived while his parents broke up, the woman who embraced him so tight she bruised him, is dead now. Not a day has passed when he has not felt her absence. She is dead, but he is nineteen years old, and alive and inhabiting space on the earth, getting As at Harvard, walking on a beach in the moonlight without any time constriction. He will never marry; he knows that now. The water looks like liquid pewter. He kicks his shoes off and, barefooted, enters the salty waters. The white waves that mark the sandbar are clearly visible in the darkness. He feels dirty, smells the cigar smoke on his clothes. He strips naked, placing the cufflinks safely in his pants pocket, and leaves his clothes on the strand. When he wades into the big white-fringed waves, the water is a cold surprise. He swims, feels clean again. Perhaps he will leave tomorrow, call the airline, change his flight, go back to Cambridge.

When he reaches the white waves, he is relieved. The water is deeper, the waves angrier now that it is night. He can rest here before the return swim to the shore. He lowers his feet to feel the sand. Waves thrash over his head, knocking him back into the deep water. He cannot find solid ground. His heart is beating fast, he swallows water, goes farther out to find the shallowest place. He never meant to drink all that champagne. He never meant to go swimming in the first place. All he wanted was to wash the evening off him. He struggles for the longest time, goes underwater, believing it will be easier if he comes up only for air. He sees the lighted condominiums on the shore. Out of nowhere comes the thought of his grandmother, who after coming all the way, and with only an hour to spend, would not get into the water, even though she was a strong, river swimmer. When he asked her why, she said she just didn't know how deep it was. Where the deep started, or where it ended. The young man floats on the surface, then slowly makes his way back to the lighted condominiums on the shore. It is a long way off, but the penthouse lights are clear against the sky. When he reaches the shallow water, he crawls on his belly and collapses on the sand. He is breathing hard and looking around for his clothes, but the tide has taken them away. He imagines the first species that crawled out of the sea, the amount of courage it took to sustain life on land. He thinks of the young men in Cambridge, his stepfather saying Harvard, like Harvard is his name, his mother's diamonds winking like fake stars, and his wish for an ordinary life.

Lewis Robinson
(Born in Massachusetts, 1972)

Still in his early thirties, Lewis Robinson lives in the state of Maine where he grew up. This story, "Ride", appeared in his 2003 debut collection, *Officer Friendly*. After graduating from the University of Iowa creative writing program, Robinson worked as John Irving's assistant for two years, drove a truck for Sotheby's in New York, and now supposedly makes his living as a sea urchin diver (summers) and a truck driver (winters).

Most of Robinson's stories are set in Maine, and each of his characters is a little odd in the head in his or her own way, as a result of which you come away from his books wondering if all the people who live in Maine are just a little bit odd in the head (which couldn't possibly be the case). *Officer Friendly* contains another birthday story "The Toast", which is also delightful, and I recommend it to anyone who enjoys "Ride".

Ride

BY LEWIS ROBINSON

In his room at home, Alden keeps a picture of his dad wearing hunting clothes, yellow and brown brush camouflage print with bloodstains on the knees. He's standing in a field, leaning against an old car that's been abandoned there, a large black sedan from the forties propped up on its axles. He rests against the car holding four woodcock, two in each hand. The sky hangs gray and the grass in the field is matted down flat. His shotgun, barrel open, lies on the hood of the car. His cheeks are red and his sideburns are long and full.

They're in the Adirondacks now, headed to Plattsburgh, New York, in his dad's forty-foot Freightliner. Looking at his watch, his dad pulls the airhorn at exactly midnight, bleeding the tanks until the pressure alarm goes off. Alden holds his hands over his ears. He tries to follow the noise as it travels through the woods, reflects off cliffs, wakes up animals, and comes to rest someplace far away – by a frozen pond, maybe, or in a field of snow.

"There it is," his dad says. "Happy birthday."

As they accelerate through curves, Alden can feel the truck's trailer hanging empty behind them – a spotless chamber which his father calls "the chapel." All they're hauling is a pine crate, suitcase-sized, which is strapped to the back wall. His father's voice, the smell of tobacco and sweat and potato chips and coffee – all of this feels immediate and slightly unreal. He hasn't lived with his dad for a long time – his parents split eight years ago.

"Aldie," his dad says, lighting a Winston and squeezing it in his lips, inhaling deeply. "Sixteen – that's a big one. It's when you take off the training wheels."

When his father asked him to go on the trip, he could have said no politely, apologetically, as he had many times in the past, but Alden was beginning to see the advantages of time spent with his father. They'd gotten to the point where they were so unknown to each other that their visits felt adventurous. They'd eat together maybe twice a year, when his father was running a job up I-95. His dad would call a day ahead, and they'd meet at the Miss Somesville Diner, where his father would tell stories and Alden would order a steak, laugh at the right times, pretend to be a man. His mother drove him to the diner, always deciding at the last minute how much time Alden could spend there – sometimes two hours, sometimes only forty-five minutes. When his time was up, she'd be waiting in her car at the edge of the parking lot, near the newspaper vending machines. It had been nine months since he'd last seen his father, and this time, his dad suggested they meet in New York, run a job upstate, then spend his birthday together. Alden said yes right away.

His father picked him up just outside Grand Central Station, and they'd driven the Freightliner up Madison Avenue, passing polished granite facades, gold and mirrored storefronts, before turning on Eighty-third Street toward Central Park, rolling down a ramp to the Metropolitan Museum's loading dock. There, men in white smocks and cotton gloves ducked under lowering gates. Phones were ringing in every direction. Two security guards with guns in their holsters were stooped over, rolling a small pine box onto the Freightliner. On each side of the box, the museum had stamped the word EXCLUSIVE in two-inch red letters, meaning it was a point-to-point job, during which no other deliveries could be made. Underneath these letters, someone had written "RAMSEY, WILLIAM. PLATTSBURGH, NEW YORK."

"Maybe it's the Mona Lisa," his dad said, winking.

They are just an hour from Plattsburgh when snow begins to swirl on the windshield. The rainbow of dashboard gauges – fluorescent reds, oranges, and greens – glows off his father's face, and the heating unit for the trailer rumbles above them. Alden feels full of hope, because it's warm in the cab, and the road is smooth and well lit by the headlights, and he anticipates stopping for junk food – all those truck-stop choices thrill him, even when he's not hungry. Also, his ass doesn't hurt yet. And it's his birthday.

The only catch is that he's not comfortable shooting the breeze with his dad – the diner is an easier venue. There, his father could entertain Alden by flirting with the waitress, for which his dad's strategy was always the same. He'd ask her to sit down on the stool next to them when she took their order, and if she was young, he'd ask where she went to high school, and he'd pretend to know her teachers if she mentioned their names. If she was older, he'd ask about her kids, and maybe even her husband. "You can relax with us," he'd say. "We won't make you work too hard."

In the truck, where there are fewer distractions, Alden is forced to make conversation. He asks, "You remember being sixteen?"

"Well," he says, smiling, "the thing was, I was built for that age. I lived on my own and I didn't have very many concerns. I washed dishes for my rent money." His dad has a tendency to speak this way, as though he were answering questions on a talk show.

"Where'd you wash dishes?"

"You know. One of those places."

Then it's quiet again. Alden glances at his father, at his graying red hair and the wrinkles where he squints.

It's hard for Alden to believe they were in the city earlier that day – it feels like weeks ago. Alden stares at the lines on the highway, unwavering in the truck's super-charged headlights.

"You should have seen how many Botero sculptures I hauled last week, Aldie," his dad says. "Thing is, a Botero is like a Buick, and I hauled fourteen of the suckers. They're these big shiny black sculptures. They're all really fat. His birds are fat, and he makes fat ladies, fat cats, fat kings and queens. If he does a dog, it's this massive thing, as big as an elephant. It's a simple equation. I envy the man. I mean, God bless him, people love his work. I think it's because these big fat things are so recognizable –

which means even dumb fuckers can say, 'Oh look! It's a Botero.' Maybe I should have been an artist. Those sculptures are worth a fortune." He lights a cigarette.

"I thought you wanted to be a hit man," says Alden. So far on the trip, his father has said he'd make a shrewd lawyer, an enterprising manager of a fast food restaurant, one hell of an astronaut.

"It would be perfect, really. No one would expect that from me," he says, laughing. "Your mother might expect it, but she's the only one. She knows what I'm capable of." What his mother has told Alden is that she loved him, but that he was too much of a dreamer, too stubborn to live with. Whenever she speaks of him, Alden knows she's holding a lot back. He remembers when he was eight, his father decided he'd make his fortune by raising llamas, and that for a while he had seventeen of them, which he kept in a rented paddock in Point Allison. He would go on and on about the virtues of the species, lecturing Alden and his mother at the dinner table. They're smart and independent and they have an uncanny sense of personal space, he'd say. His mother hated this talk, Alden remembers, and when seven of them died of a rare blood disorder and his father sold a necklace of hers to buy five more, that was it. He was gone two months later. The llama episode is the main reason his mother doesn't want Alden to spend time with him; she doesn't want Alden to pick up any of his habits.

Without announcement, his father exits the highway onto a thinner road. When they veer down into a hollow, near a stream that parallels the road, it's easy to feel how light the truck is, how empty. The brakes don't strain on the downhill, and a small burst of diesel heaves them up the other side. The trailer leans against the turns.

With all the dips and curves, Alden can tell they're in the mountains, but he can't see the peaks – they're hidden by the forest, and by the snow, which is falling much more heavily now. Alden remembers reading somewhere that the Adirondacks are an old mountain range, older than the Rockies, big windswept piles of granite. This gives him an empty, paralyzed feeling, all those old rocks, like the time he saw a late-night show on the Pyramids and couldn't get his head around the idea of all those Egyptians being dead for thousands of years. He tries to shake the thought by imagining the next truck stop – racks and racks of quilted plaid shirts, Silhouette Lady mud flaps, biker magnets, Road Warrior sew-on patches. A smorgasbord of beef jerky.

"You ever talk to people when you're on the road?" asks Alden.

"How do you mean?"

"If you're at a truck stop, or at a restaurant, or – I don't know, wherever – you ever chat people up, get to know them?" asks Alden. He wonders this about his dad – he's never heard about his friends, and the only people he's watched him talk to are waitresses.

"Sometimes I talk to people. A lot of the time, though, it's just a letdown. When you think about it, there aren't many people out there worth knowing."

They pass a sign announcing the Elizabethtown Motel and Restaurant: COME TO WHERE THE COMFORT IS! Alden sees mobile homes in the periphery of the headlights, dark rectangles strewn irregularly by the side of the highway. His father downshifts and begins to slow the truck. Up ahead there's a package store with gas pumps, but the lights are out.

"I think it's closed," says Alden.

"Yup," says his dad. Alden can feel the truck sliding in the snow, and his father eases off the brakes. He pulls up next to the diesel pumps, which are dark. The store has a porch in front, with a phone booth.

"I guess you're old enough to get all the details on this," his father says. "You okay with that?"

"Sure," says Alden.

"That's just because you have no idea what I'm talking about," he says, exhaling, pushing a hand through his hair.

"What?"

"Well, give me a second, for Christ sake."

"Okay," says Alden.

"Here's the thing. We're going to wait at this store for a guy I know. He's going to help us with this job. Help us get this painting we're hauling up to Canada."

"It's not going to Plattsburgh?"

"Nope. It's supposed to be going there. But that's where the old man gets smart." He turns off the engine. "What we're going to do is make it look like we've been held up." He glances at his watch. "Williamson's supposed to be here by now."

"How?"

His father looks annoyed. "He's driving his car down from Montreal."

"I mean how are you going to make it look like we've been held up?"

"We don't really have to do anything. We just have to tell them that someone crazy put a gun to my head."

Alden's confused. "Why'd you stop at this store in the first place?"

"It's where we're meeting Williamson."

"I know. But why . . . you know . . . in the story you're going to tell the cops?"

"It doesn't matter. Maybe I'll tell them I didn't think it was closed."

"And that the robbers just happened to be here?"

"Hell, it doesn't matter. I'm not supposed to know anything, right? If have some elaborate theory, the cops will smell that, right? Maybe the robbers were following me. Maybe they were following me all the way from New York."

"Oh," says Alden.

"And don't you worry. This money's for you. It's not all for me, you know. I've been paying every bill your mom sends me for the last eight years, that's been fine. But now I want to set us up for a while, okay?"

His father clicks on the radio.

"Have you ever done this before?" asks Alden.

"You think that matters?" says his dad.

"No, not really. I'm just curious."

"Well, it does matter. Because no, I haven't done it before, which is probably what'll make it work."

Alden opens his door and gets out. He looks up in the sky, closes his eyes, and feels the big snowflakes against his face, in his eyelashes. None of what's happening feels real. It doesn't seem dangerous, or exciting. Already it feels like a story he'll be telling his mom. With his eyes closed, he wants to see only darkness but he sees flashes of light, though when he opens his eyes again, it's the same quiet scene, almost pretty in the snow: this dead store, the faint sound of country music coming from the truck.

Then the pay phone rings, which seems impossible. He looks at his father, who sits unmoving in the truck, listening to the music. Two more rings go by before Alden goes to the truck, opens the door on his father's side and says, "This phone out here is ringing."

"Why don't you get it?" says his father.

"I want you to pick it up," says Alden.

"Jesus," says his father, hopping down from his seat into the snow, then running over to the phone. He talks for only a few seconds, then slams the phone down. He jogs back to the truck.

"Okay," he says. "He went off the road outside La Prairie. We need to take it up to Canada ourselves."

Alden has never been outside the United States, and while he has little faith in his father's plan, he likes the idea of crossing into foreign territory. Twenty minutes later, they're at the border, driving under a row of tall, pooling fluorescent lights. They roll up to a booth at the same level as the truck's cab, high above the road. Low scrub and dwarfed trees cover the land around them, and the lights make everything sharp.

"Aldie," his dad says, sighing. "This is what we call a D-plus operation – real junior varsity." His mother says he gets this way sometimes because he thinks he knows how things should be done correctly – it's the marine in him. Even when waiting in line at the DMV, or going to the town hall to get a burn permit, it's the exact same thing.

"Bonjour, hello," says the woman in the booth, without looking up. "United States citizens, both of you?" Her well-enunciated English is fringed by an accent.

"This is my son here. Sixteen years old today. Well, yes, we're both Americans. Yes ma'am," his dad says, handing her the truck papers.

"And what are you bringing to Canada?" she asks.

His father glances at Alden, then turns back toward the woman. "Military dominance," he says. "Louisiana jazz, Fenway Park, the Chevy Silverado." Then, after a dramatic pause, "The Grand Canyon." He laughs. "Just kidding, Ma'am, of course."

Alden has heard this list, and others like it, before. The woman is wearing a tan uniform and looks about his mom's age; she has sharp eyebrows and short brown hair. "Excuse me?"

"We're empty, ma'am," he says. "We're going up to Montreal to get some seafood."

"Sir, the climate-control unit for your trailer is engaged," she says. She sounds relaxed, with the calm assurance you get when you have the authority of an entire country behind you.

"Is it, ma'am?" his dad asks.

"Full blast," she says.

"I better turn it off. Don't want to heat something that's not back there."

"On the left, there, is Import," she says, pointing. "Back into loading dock three and open your trailer. An officer will be with you shortly."

Alden's father releases the air brake, and they roll from the window. "That's the other thing I'm bringing to Canada," he says. "A goddamn sense of humor."

They pull into Import, open the trailer doors, and back their way into a loading dock. Alden is out in the cold, giving hand signals. Flapping of the hand means keep coming, straight ahead; then he holds his hands apart, showing his dad how much room there is before his bumper meets the dock. With its own diesel engine fed by the main fuel tanks, the reefer unit on the Freightliner is a workhorse. It pumps hot air from the trailer into the loading dock.

His dad sets the air brakes, a loud crack, then a hiss. Now the snow is falling in a fine mist, a spray of sugar. It's cold weather snow, the kind that could last for days. The seam between the trailer and the Import bay leaks some heat to Alden, so he stands close. Up by the cab, he sees his dad's shoulder in the long vertical mirror. He jogs up to the cab and climbs in the passenger side.

"Aldie, I need you to keep lookout for me. Go wait on the slab back there. I'm going to get that crate from the chapel."

"That seems like a bad idea," says Alden.

"Like you would know? They won't see anything. Aldie. Don't worry."

"I say we turn around now, Dad. Before this gets any worse."

"Come on now," his dad says, pleading. "It's not your ass, it's mine."

The parking lot by Import is one of the best-lit places Alden has ever seen. There are lampposts – tall, as bright as lighthouse lanterns – every fifteen feet. The snow is filling the air now, churning, and the sky is thick black above the tops of the lampposts. The snow falls brightly by the bulbs, and as the light spreads out toward the ground, the snow is less visible, but three or four inches have already fallen. He gets out of the truck.

The snow burns his arms but feels good in his hair, which is hot from the heat of the cab. He walks back to the end of the truck and stands by the warm draft again. There's a truck in the next bay, and two men sit on the separating concrete slab. They speak a singsong version of French, lots of ups and downs. Instead of "oui," they say "whey." They're laughing loudly, shaking, occasionally clapping their hands. One of them is wearing a black wool hat which fits tightly on his head, and the other has pockmarked skin and gray spiked hair. They are smoking cigarettes with gloves on.

"Bonjour," Alden says to them.

"Hello," the one with the spiked hair says, and his companion nods, silently.

"Great spot," says Alden.

"Whey," they both say, laughing some more and nodding. The guy with spiked hair says, "It gets even better when Mr. Immigration comes here, sticks his gun in your guts, and blows off your kidneys."

This makes both the men laugh again. There's no burning on Alden's arms anymore, they're numb. The one with the gray spiked hair takes a fresh cigarette out of his pack and points it in Alden's direction.

"Merci," Alden says, extending a pink arm that doesn't feel part of him. Then the man walks up to his cab and comes back with a plaid wool shirt and gloves.

"You from Florida, tough man?" he says as he hands Alden the clothes. The one in the hat says something in French to the one with spiked hair – it seems he doesn't like that these clothes have been offered to Alden. But they say nothing more, so while holding the cigarette in his mouth, Alden puts on the shirt and the gloves – which smell like air freshener, something floral.

"Maine. I'm just catching a ride with this guy," he says, pointing toward his father's truck. "I've been on the road for a few days."

"Does he stop to let you take a piss?" asks the man with spiked hair. "Because Reggie, he doesn't stop to let me piss." Alden looks at Reggie, who is smiling with his arms folded across his chest.

"He lets me," says Alden.

"Well, mister, you're one lucky bastard," says the man with spiked hair.

Alden hasn't smoked many cigarettes before, and this one burns stale and strong. He tries not to inhale too much until he's gotten used to the smoke in his mouth. Ready, he sucks deep, holds it, then opens his mouth and lets it drift thick over his teeth. His eyes water and his vision changes and he almost falls over, but he realizes he hasn't moved. The snow coming into the loading dock is gentle, landing on heads and mustaches silently. Alden looks back out at the lampposts, shining as brilliantly as ever, then tosses the cigarette into the snow, where it blackens. Again he sees his dad's shoulder in the vertical mirror. His dad opens the door and waves Alden up to the cab.

"Christ. They might have seen me," his dad says. His face is red from the heat of the cab, and from the excitement. "I saw where the camera was, and I stayed out of its way. But then somebody came out onto the . . . " He stops, wrinkling his nose. "Aldie, were you smoking?" he asks.

"Nope. Those guys back there, they lent me this shirt," he says, still pumped with nicotine.

"Aldie, we need to take control of the situation," his father says, out of breath. "That's exactly what we're going to do. It's what you and I are, Aldie. We're take-control types. You're sixteen, bub – time to show the world what you're made of." Alden feels the pine suitcase behind his seat, where it's lodged, hidden.

The Immigration officer is in the back of the truck. Alden hears his boots. His dad puts a Winston in his teeth and lights it. A minute later, the officer's at the window.

"Extinguish the cigarette," the officer says. He has a footlong silver flashlight which he shines in Alden's eyes. "What's your business in Canada?" he asks.

"Just visiting," Alden's dad says.

"Sir, let me tell you something about my job," says the officer. He has a neatly trimmed moustache and a thin mouth. "I'm cold and I'm tired. I'm at the end of my twelve-hour shift. You're not in Canada yet. You're with me, and you'll answer me directly. "

"What I was going to tell you – "

"Am I clear?"

" – is that we're picking up some artwork in Canada."

"Am I clear?"

"Sure," his father says. "You're clear."

"The next shift will do the cab inspection. Officer McKenna will be with you shortly."

His father sighs. "Jesus, you're not going to take a knife to my seats, are you? I've had that done by you guys before."

"Stay in the cab," says the officer. Then he walks away.

"Have a wonderful evening," says his father, after the officer has left.

He hops out of the cab and Alden follows him. They walk into the Import lobby, which is lit only by vending machines and a red glowing exit sign. Alden scans a humming candy machine: every dispenser is filled with the same kind of toffee. His dad goes to the pay phone, and Alden heads for the men's room.

The floor by the toilets is muddy from boots and urine. There's no heat in the bathroom; his breath steams and the sink fixtures are painfully cold. Alden looks at his face in the mirror. His skin is white but his nose stands out pink. Sixteen, he says to himself. A cigarette-smoking, French-speaking son of a blundering outlaw.

Alden walks out of the bathroom, and through the window he sees the other truck pull out of Import, and as it turns, the rear wheels of the trailer slide across the snow-covered asphalt, fishtailing gently. Then the trailer pulls straight.

Alden walks past his father, and when he gets outside he jogs across the lot toward the moving truck. In the snow, it's silent. Alden sees its brake lights flash – a bright, hopeful red – then his feet come out from under him and he lands hard on the asphalt, first his elbows, then the right side of his ribs, then his right knee. He reminds himself it would have hurt much more had there not been snow – but then again, he wouldn't have slipped had the asphalt been dry. The truck is idling, waiting for him. He runs to the passenger side, where the man with spiked hair has rolled down the window.

"Nice stunt back there," says the man, laughing. "Très bien."

"I didn't give you back your stuff," says Alden.

"No?" he says. "That's okay, those things are Reggie's." He jabs a thumb in his partner's direction.

Alden hears a spill of French words from Reggie, whom he can't see.

"Oh, what a generous guy," says the man, laughing. "Reggie says you can have them. He found them in the trash at a truck stop in Iberville."

"You guys have space?" asks Alden. "It's fine if you don't, I can wait, but that other rig's being delayed, and I'm hoping to keep moving."

"No problem, we can give you a ride," he says. "You ride in the trailer, okay? You fit back there. It's dark, but we have only one hour before Montreal. It's good back there, plenty of room."

"Sounds fine," says Alden.

The man opens his door and swings his legs around, then hops down out of the cab, landing quietly on the snow. He walks with Alden to the back of the truck, where he opens the padlock and one of the hinged doors. "I'll give you a second to find your way, then I close you up," he says. "Take a good look around before it gets dark."

Inside the trailer doors are three tall lamps strapped to the wall, a grandfather clock, a bookshelf, four mattresses on their sides, stacked together. The rest of the stuff inside is too far back to see. Alden puts a foot on the bumper, and just as he's pulling himself up, he hears a high whistle from across the parking lot. He looks toward the Import bay and sees his father, waving him back. He stares at his father, who then starts waving with greater urgency.

"Oh," says Alden. "Looks like he's ready now. Maybe I'll just go with him."

"Okay," says the man, who slams the door closed.

"Sorry," says Alden.

The man clicks the padlock shut. "Hey, he lets you stop to piss, right?" says the man. "You're better off, mon frère." The man walks back up to the cab, hops inside, and the truck pulls away.

When Alden gets back to the Import dock, he gets into his father's truck and his father leans toward him. "You wouldn't believe it," he whispers, smiling. "These guys are total amateurs. This last Gomer looks behind the seat, sees the crate, doesn't even ask me what's in it."

"Oh yeah?"

"Must have thought it was a toolbox. I didn't even flinch, Aldie. Not one bit."

His father releases the air brakes and pulls slowly out of the bay. "I talked to Williamson again," says his father. "He called it off. I guess there's no reason to push it tonight." Then he carves a large U-turn. At the American gate, they roll up to a booth where an officer with an American flag on his shoulder has his chin down on his chest with his eyes closed. Alden has forgotten about the time, but he figures it must be nearly three in the morning.

"I missed my exit, back down in Plattsburgh," his dad says.

"One minute," the officer says. He mutters a few words into an intercom mounted to the wall, clicking it with his thumb, looking absently at the truck. Then he says, "You were just headed into Canada?"

"No, sir," says his father.

"You weren't just headed into Canada," says the man.

"Yes," says Alden, almost too loudly. "Into Canada. Yes sir."

"Yes?" asks the officer.

"We were, but the pickup got canceled," says Alden. "They called it off because of the weather."

"Sir?" asks the officer.

Alden's father nods and says, "That's right."

"Sorry for the mixup, sir," says Alden.

"I recommend you get off the road soon, with all this snow," says the officer.

"Will do," says Alden.

"Go ahead," says the officer, waving them on.

Any snow that momentarily settles in the spruce trees soon swirls up in gusts of wind. Then his father lights a Winston. "Let me do the talking next time," he says, finally. He breathes out smoke like a sleuth.

"I didn't want you to mess things up again," says Alden.

"Oh, thank you *so much*," his dad says. "Thanks for saving me, son. You're my savior."

"Just so you know," says Alden, "I was saving myself, not you." He says this without thinking, and it makes him go numb, so he squeezes his arms and tries to stare at the lines on the highway again. He and his father are quiet for the rest of the trip.

When they arrive at the motel, his father puts the pine box in the trailer and keeps the heater running.

The room is dimly lit, the wallpaper is watercolored deer and moose standing in brown and yellow reeds. There is only one bed, king-size, and Alden climbs into it next to his father. When they turn out the lamp, light from the parking lot glows through the curtains. In the faint light of the room, he catches a glimpse of his father, who has the sheets pulled up into his armpits, his arms resting above the covers. His father says, "I guess your birthday didn't work out quite like I planned. I was thinking we'd rent some skates in Montreal. Go out on the river."

"It's all right," says Alden.

"Next time," says his father.

"Okay," says Alden, but Alden knows any chance of this happening has past.

Then his father sits up, clicks on the lamp. "I have an

idea," he says. In his white briefs, he pulls on his boots, grabs his keys, and opens the door to the motel room. Then he walks out into the snow. In a few minutes, he's back, pink-chested, clutching the pine box under one arm. He lays it on the bed, unscrewing the side of it with a Swiss Army knife on his key chain. He removes the panel, slips the painting from its foam sheath, then removes the glassine wrapping.

Alden props a few pillows behind his head and watches as his dad, in boots and underwear, places the painting in front of the TV.

A tree frog fills most of the canvas – it's huge and wet-looking, settled in the grass. The sun on its back makes its skin appear white. The frog isn't realistic, but the light is. "Jesus," says his father. "That's some crazy shit right there."

"You like it?" asks Alden.

"I like it fine," says his father. "You?"

"Sure."

"Not what I was expecting, but still pretty nice. I was convinced it was going to be something else."

"The Mona Lisa?" asks Alden.

"Hey, don't be a smart-ass," says his dad, with his arms folded on his chest, staring at the painting. "I was ninety-nine percent sure it was this little Cézanne number, with apples in it."

"Good thing you didn't steal this one," says Alden.

"You got that right, soldier," says his father.

"I mean, the frog's pretty good, but if you weren't expecting it –"

"– it's a whole different operation. Right you are," says his father. "Hey, maybe we should go up to Canada anyway. Tomorrow. Just for the hell of it."

"I'm ready to get home," says Alden.

"Okay," says his father, staring intently at the painting. "I guess it's time to get some sleep." He climbs back under the covers. After turning off the lamp for the second time he says, "Well, happy birthday."

"Thanks," says Alden, and in the dark he listens for the truck's heating unit, but it's off now.

As he tries to sleep, Alden remembers the day when his father left Maine – he had taken Alden out for breakfast, though he can't remember the conversation. Alden suspects his dad had been apologetic. He had to have been. And Alden went with him to Point Allison, to get the money for the llamas – he'd sold them. (Alden remembers the llamas, perhaps not from that particular visit to Point Allison, but he remembers the way they walked slowly in their paddock, looking curious and dignified.) And then there was the moment when his dad pressed the money into Alden's hand, a small smooth fold of bills, asking him to deliver it to Alden's mother. He had liked that. He hadn't known the full meaning of the gesture, but he knew it was a good thing, that it would improve the situation, and he liked that he could be the deliverer. He liked being a part of the exchange. Alden doesn't know when he'd started to home in on loneliness. It had snuck up on him, really. (He used to feel a touch of surprise when he looked at himself in the mirror, as though most of the time he was unaware he was separate from the rest of the world.) In some ways, this feels right – in the daytime, he is invigorated by solitude. But in the motel room, he just feels lonely. With his father sleeping next to him, Alden feels a new kind of sadness, as though he's got a secret which he will never tell.

Haruki Murakami
(Born in Kyoto, 1949)

And finally, to round out the book, I include a birth-day story of my own, one written specifically for inclusion in the Japanese edition of this anthology.

Do you remember what you were doing on the day you turned 20 (or 21, the more important birthday in many countries)? I remember my own twentieth birthday very well. January 12, 1969 was a raw, thinly-overcast day in Tokyo, and (though I can hardly believe it now) I was waiting on tables in a coffee shop after lectures. I had wanted the day off but couldn't find anyone to take my place. Not a single pleasant thing happened to me right up to the very end of the day in what seemed (at the time) like an omen of all the years to come. Like me, the birth-day girl of this story looks as if she's going to have a lonely, nothing-much kind of twentieth birthday. The sun goes down, and it even starts to rain. Could there be, as Grace Paley might say, some kind of "enormous change at the last minute" waiting for her?

Birthday Girl

BY HARUKI MURAKAMI

Translated from the Japanese by Jay Rubin

She waited on tables as usual that day, her twentieth birthday. She always worked on Fridays, but if things had gone according to plan on that particular Friday, she would have taken the night off. The other part-time girl had agreed to switch shifts with her as a matter of course: being screamed at by an angry chef while lugging pumpkin gnocchi and seafood *fritto* to customers' tables was no way to spend one's twentieth birthday. But the other girl had aggravated a cold and gone to bed with unrelenting diarrhoea and a temperature of 104°, so she ended up working after all at short notice.

She found herself trying to comfort the sick girl, who had called to apologise. "Don't worry about it," she said. "I wasn't going to do anything special anyway, even if it is my twentieth birthday."

And in fact she was not all that disappointed. One reason was the terrible argument she had had a few days earlier with the boyfriend who was supposed to be with her that night. They had been going out since high school. The argument had started from nothing much but it had taken an unexpected turn for the worse until it became a long and bitter shouting match – one bad enough, she was pretty sure, to have snapped their long-standing ties once and for all. Something inside her had turned rock-hard and died. He had not called her since the bust-up, and she was not about to call him.

Her workplace was one of the better known Italian restaurants in the tony Roppongi district of Tokyo. It had been in business since the late '60s and, while its cuisine was hardly cutting edge, its high reputation was fully justified. It had many regular customers and they were never disappointed. The dining room had a calm, relaxed atmosphere without a hint of pushiness. Rather than a young crowd, the restaurant drew an older clientele which included some famous actors and writers.

The two full-time waiters worked six days a week. She and the other part-time waitress were students who took turns working three days each. In addition there was one floor manager and, at the register, a skinny, middle-aged woman who had apparently been there since the restaurant opened – literally sitting in the one place, it seemed, like some gloomy old character from *Little Dorrit*. She had exactly two functions: to accept payment from the customers and to answer the phone. She spoke only when necessary and always wore the same black dress. There was something cold and hard about her: if you set her afloat on the night-time sea she would probably sink any boat that happened to ram her.

The floor manager was perhaps in his late forties. Tall and broad-shouldered, his build suggested that he had been a sportsman in his youth, but excess flesh was now beginning to accumulate on his belly and chin. His short, stiff hair was thinning at the crown, and an ageing bachelor smell clung to him – like newspaper that had been stored in a drawer with cough drops. She had a bachelor uncle who smelled like that.

The manager always wore a black suit, white shirt and bow tie – not a snap-on bow tie, but the real thing, tied by hand. It was a point of pride for him that he could tie it perfectly without looking in a mirror. He performed his duties adroitly day after day. They consisted of checking the arrival and departure of guests and keeping abreast of the reservation schedule, of knowing the names of regular customers and greeting them with a smile, lending a respectful ear to any complaints that might arise, giving expert advice on wines and overseeing the work of the waiters and waitresses. It was also his special task to deliver dinner to the room of the restaurant's owner.

*

"The owner had his own room on the sixth floor of the same building where the restaurant was," she said. "An apartment or office or something."

Somehow she and I had got onto the subject of our twentieth birthdays – what sort of day it had been for each of us. Most people remember the day they turned 20. Hers had been more than ten years earlier.

"He never, ever showed his face in the restaurant, though. The only one who saw him was the manager. It was exclusively *his* job to deliver the owner's dinner to him. None of the other employees even knew what he looked like."

"So, basically, the owner was getting home delivery from his own restaurant."

"Right," she said. "Every night at eight, the manager had to bring dinner to the owner's room. It was the restaurant's busiest time, so having the manager disappear just then was always a problem for us, but there was no way around it because that was the way it had always been done. They'd load the dinner onto one of those trolleys that hotels use for room service, the manager would push it into the lift wearing a respectful look on his face, and 15 minutes later he'd come back, empty-handed. Then, an hour later, he'd go up again and bring down the trolley with the empty plates and glasses. Every day, like clockwork. I thought it was really weird the first time I saw it happen. It was like some kind of religious ritual, you know? But after a while I got used to it and I never gave it a second thought."

*

The owner always had chicken. The recipe and the vegetable side dishes were a little different every day, but the main dish was always chicken. A young chef once told her that he had tried sending up roast chicken every day for a week just to see what would happen, but there was never any complaint. A chef wants to try different ways of preparing things, of course, and each new chef would challenge himself with every technique for chicken that he could think of. They'd make elegant sauces, they'd try chicken from different suppliers, but none of their efforts elicited a response: they might just as well have been throwing pebbles into an empty cave. In the end, every one of them gave up and prepared a run-of-the-mill chicken dish for the owner every day. That's all that was ever asked of them.

Work started as usual on her twentieth birthday, November 17. It had been raining on and off since the afternoon and pouring since early evening. At 5 p.m. the manager gathered the employees together to explain the day's specials. Servers were required to memorise them word for word and not use written notes: veal Milanese, pasta topped with sardines and cabbage, chestnut mousse. Sometimes the manager would play the rôle of a customer and test them with questions. Then came the employees' meal: waiters in *this* restaurant were not going to have growling stomachs as they took diners' orders!

The restaurant opened its doors at six o'clock, but, due to the downpour, guests were slow to arrive and several reservations were simply cancelled. Ladies didn't want their dresses ruined by the rain. The manager walked around, tight-lipped, and the waiters killed time polishing the salt cellars and pepper mills or chatting with the chef about cooking. She surveyed the dining room with its single couple at a table and listened to the harpsichord music flowing discreetly from ceiling speakers. A deep smell of late autumn rain worked its way into the restaurant.

It was after 7.30 when the manager started feeling sick. He stumbled over to a chair and sat there for a while, holding his stomach as if he had just been shot. A greasy sweat clung to his forehead. "I think I'd better go to hospital," he muttered. For him to be taken ill was a most unusual occurrence: he had never missed a day since he started working in the restaurant over ten years earlier. It was another point of pride for him that he had never been absent through illness or injury, but his painful grimace made it clear that he was in very bad shape.

She stepped outside with an umbrella and hailed a taxi. One of the waiters held the manager steady and climbed into the car with him to take him to a nearby hospital. Before ducking into the taxi the manager said to her hoarsely, "I want you to take a dinner up to room 604 at eight o'clock. All you have to do is ring the bell, say 'Your dinner is here,' and leave it."

"That's room 604, right?" she said.

"At eight o'clock," he repeated. "On the dot." He grimaced again, climbed in, and the taxi drove away.

The rain showed no signs of letting up after the manager had left and customers arrived only at long intervals. No more than one or two tables were occupied at a time, so if the manager and one waiter had to be absent, this was a good time for it to happen. Things could get so busy that it was not unusual for even the full compliment of staff to have trouble coping.

When the owner's meal was ready at eight o'clock, she pushed the room-service trolley into the lift and rode up to the sixth floor. It was the usual meal for him: a half-bottle of red wine with the cork loosened, a thermal pot of coffee, a chicken entrée with steamed vegetables, rolls and butter. The heavy aroma of cooked chicken quickly filled the lift. It mingled with the smell of the rain. Water droplets dotted the lift floor, suggesting that someone with a wet umbrella had recently been aboard.

She pushed the trolley down the corridor, bringing it to a stop in front of the door marked "604". She double-checked her memory: 604. That was it. She cleared her throat and pressed the doorbell.

There was no answer. She stood there for a good 20 seconds. Just as she was thinking of pressing the bell again, the door opened inwards and a skinny old man appeared. He was shorter than she was, by some four or five inches. He wore a dark suit and a tie. Against his white shirt, the tie stood out distinctly, its brownish-yellow colouring like withered leaves. He made a very clean impression, his clothes perfectly pressed, his white hair smoothed down: he looked as though he was about to go out for the night to some sort of function. The wrinkles that creased his brow made her think of deep ravines in an aerial photograph.

"Your dinner, sir," she said in a husky voice, then quietly cleared her throat again. Her voice grew husky whenever she was tense.

"Dinner?"

"Yes, sir. The manager felt sick all of a sudden. I had to take his place today. Your meal, sir."

"Oh, I see," the old man said, almost as if talking to himself, his hand still perched on the doorknob. "Sick, eh? You don't say."

"His stomach started to hurt him all of a sudden. He went to hospital. He thinks he might have appen-dicitis."

"Oh, that's not good," the old man said, running his fingers along the wrinkles of his forehead. "Not good at all."

She cleared her throat again. "Shall I bring in your meal, sir?" she asked.

"Ah yes, of course," the old man said. "Yes, of course, if you wish. That's fine with me."

If I wish? she thought. What a strange way to put it. What am I supposed to wish?

The old man opened the door the rest of the way and she wheeled the trolley inside. The floor had short, grey wall-to-wall carpeting with no area for removing shoes. The first room was like a large study, as though the apartment were more a workplace than a residence. The window looked out on the nearby Tokyo Tower, its steel skeleton outlined in lights. There was a large desk by the window and beside it, a sofa and two leather armchairs. The old man pointed to the Formica coffee table in front of the sofa. She arranged his meal on the table: white napkin and silverware, coffee pot and cup, wine and wineglass, bread and butter and the plate of chicken and vegetables.

"If you would be kind enough to set the dishes in the corridor as usual, sir, I'll come to get them in an hour."

Her words seemed to snap him out of an appreciative contemplation of his dinner. "Oh yes, of course. I'll put them in the corridor. On the trolley. In an hour. If you wish."

Yes, she replied inwardly, for the moment that is exactly what I wish. "Is there anything else I can do for you, sir?"

"No, I don't think so," he said, after a moment's consideration. He was wearing black shoes polished to a high sheen. They were small and chic. He's a stylish dresser, she thought. And he stands very straight for his age.

"Well, then, sir, I'll be getting back to work."

"No, wait just a moment," he said.

"Sir?"

"Do you think it might be possible for you to give me five minutes of your time, miss? I have something I'd like to say to you."

He was so polite in his request that it made her blush. "I . . . think it should be all right," she said. "I mean, if it really is just five minutes." He was her employer, after all. He was paying her by the hour. It was not a question of her giving or his taking her time. And this old man did not look like a person who would do anything bad to her.

"By the way, how old are you?" the old man asked, standing by the table with arms folded and looking directly into her eyes.

"I'm 20 now," she said.

"Twenty *now*," he repeated, narrowing his eyes as if peering through some kind of crack. "Twenty *now*. As of when?"

"Well, I just turned 20," she said. After a moment's hesitation, she added, "Today is my birthday, sir."

"I see," he said, rubbing his chin as if this explained a great deal for him. "Today, is it? Today is your twentieth birthday?"

She nodded.

"Your life in this world began exactly 20 years ago today."

"Yes, sir," she said, "that is correct."

"I see, I see," he said. "That's wonderful. Well, then, Happy Birthday."

"Thank you very much," she said, and it dawned on her that this was the first time all day that anyone had wished her a happy birthday. Of course, if her parents called from Oita, she might find a message from them on her answering machine when she got home from work.

"Well, well, this is certainly a cause for celebration," he said. "How about a little toast? We can drink this red wine."

"Thank you, sir, but I couldn't, I'm working now."

"Oh, what's the harm in a little sip? No-one's going to blame you if I say it's all right. Just a token drink to celebrate."

The old man slid the cork from the bottle and dribbled a little wine into his glass for her. Then he took an ordinary drinking glass from a glass-doored cabinet and poured some wine for himself.

"Happy Birthday," he said. "May you live a rich and fruitful life, and may there be nothing to cast dark shadows on it."

They clinked glasses.

May there be nothing to cast dark shadows on it: she silently repeated his remark to herself. Why had he chosen such unusual words for her birthday toast?

"Your twentieth birthday comes but once in a lifetime, miss. It's an irreplaceable day."

"Yes, sir, I know," she said, taking a cautious sip of her wine.

"And here, on your special day, you have taken the trouble to deliver my dinner to me like a kind-hearted fairy."

"Just doing my job, sir."

"But still," the old man said with a few quick shakes of the head. "But still, lovely young miss."

The old man sat in the leather chair by his desk and motioned her to the sofa. She lowered herself gingerly onto the edge of the seat, the wineglass still in her hand. Knees aligned, she tugged at her skirt, clearing her throat again. She saw raindrops tracing lines down the windowpane. The room was strangely quiet.

"Today just happens to be your twentieth birthday and on top of that you have brought me this wonderful hot meal," the old man said as if reconfirming the situation. Then he set his glass on the desktop with a little thud. "This has to be some kind of special convergence, don't you think?"

Not quite convinced, she managed a weak smile.

"Which is why," he said, touching the knot of his withered-leaf-coloured tie, "I feel it is important for me to give you a birthday present. A special birthday calls for a special commemorative gift."

Flustered, she shook her head and said, "No, please, sir, don't give it a second thought. All I did was bring your meal the way I was instructed to."

The old man raised both hands, palms towards her. "No, miss, don't you give it a second thought. The kind of 'present' I have in mind is not something tangible, not something with a price tag. To put it simply," he placed his hands on the desk and took one long, slow breath, "what I would like to do for a lovely young fairy such as you is to grant a wish you might have and to make that wish come true. Anything. Anything at all that you wish for – assuming that you *do* have such a wish."

"A wish?" she asked, her throat dry.

"Something you would like to have happen, miss. If you have a wish – one wish, I'll make it come true. That is the kind of birthday present I can give you. But you had better think about it very carefully because I can grant you only one." He raised a finger. "Just one. You can't change your mind afterwards and take it back."

She was at a loss for words. One wish? Whipped by the wind, raindrops tapped unevenly at the windowpane. As long as she remained silent, the old man looked into her eyes, saying nothing. Time marked its irregular pulse in her ears.

"I have to wish for something, and it will be granted?"

Instead of answering her question, the old man – hands still side-by-side on the desk – just smiled. He did it in the most natural and amiable way.

"Do you have a wish, miss, or not?" he asked gently.

*

"This really did happen," she said, looking straight at me. "I'm not making it up."

"Of course not," I said. She was not the sort of person to invent some goofy story out of thin air. "So . . . did you make a wish?"

She went on looking at me for a while, then released a tiny sigh. "Don't get me wrong," she said. "I wasn't taking him 100 per cent seriously myself. I mean, at 20 you're not exactly living in a fairy-tale world any more. If this was his idea of a joke, though, I had to hand it to him for coming up with it on the spot. He was a dapper old fellow with a twinkle in his eye, so I decided to play along with him. It was my twentieth birthday, after all: I thought I ought to have *something* not-so-ordinary happen to me that day. It wasn't a question of believing or not believing."

I nodded without saying anything.

"You can understand how I felt, I'm sure. My twentieth birthday was coming to an end without anything special happening, nobody wishing me a happy birthday, and all I'm doing is carrying tortellini with anchovy sauce to people's tables."

"Don't worry," I said. "I understand."

"So I made a wish."

*

The old man kept his gaze fixed on her, saying nothing, hands on the desktop. On the desk were also several thick folders that might have been account books, plus writing implements, a calendar and a lamp with a green shade. Lying amongst them, his small hands looked like another sort of desktop furnishing. The rain continued to beat against the window, the lights of Tokyo Tower filtering through the shattered drops.

The wrinkles on the old man's forehead deepened slightly. "That is your wish?"

"Yes," she said. "That is my wish."

"A bit unusual for a girl your age," he said. "I was expecting something different."

"If it's no good I can wish for something else," she said, clearing her throat. "I don't mind. I'll think of something else."

"No, no," the old man said, raising his hands and waving them like flags. "There's nothing wrong with it, nothing at all. It's just a little surprising, miss. Don't you have something else? Like, say, you want to be prettier, or more intelligent, or rich: you're okay with not wishing for something like that – something an ordinary girl would ask for?"

She took some moments to search for the right words. The old man just waited, saying nothing, his hands at rest together on the desk again.

"Of course I'd like to be prettier, or more intelligent, or rich. But I really can't imagine what would happen to me if any of those things came true. It might be more than I could handle. I still don't really know what life is all about. I don't know how it works."

"I see," the old man said, intertwining his fingers and separating them again. "I see."

"So, is my wish okay?"

"Of course," he said. "Of course. It's no trouble for me at all."

The old man suddenly fixed his eyes on a spot in the air. The wrinkles of his forehead deepened: they might have been the wrinkles of his brain itself as it concentrated on his thoughts. He seemed to be staring at something – perhaps all-but-invisible bits of down – floating in front of him. He opened his arms wide, lifted himself slightly from his chair and whipped his palms together with a dry

smack. Settling in the chair again, he slowly ran his fingertips along the wrinkles of his brow as if to soften them and
then turned to her with a gentle smile.

"That did it," he said. "Your wish has been granted."

"Already?"

"Yes, it was no trouble at all. Your wish has been
granted, lovely miss. Happy Birthday. You may go back to
work now. Don't worry, I'll put the trolley in the corridor."

She took the lift down to the restaurant. Empty-
handed now, she felt almost disturbingly light, as though
she were walking on some kind of mysterious fluff.

"Are you okay? You look spaced out," the younger
waiter said to her.

She gave him an ambiguous smile and shook her head.
"Oh, really? No, I'm fine."

"Tell me about the owner. What's he like?"

"I dunno, I didn't get a very good look at him," she
said, cutting the conversation short.

An hour later she went to bring the trolley down. It was
out in the corridor, utensils in place. She lifted the lid to
find the chicken and vegetables gone. The wine bottle and
coffee pot were empty. The door to room 604 stood there,
closed and expressionless. She stared at it for a while, feeling it might open at any moment, but it did not open. She
brought the trolley down in the lift and wheeled it to the
dish washer. The chef looked blankly at the plate: empty as
always.

*

"I never saw the owner again," she said. "Not once. The

manager turned out to have just an ordinary stomach ache and went back to delivering the owner's meal himself the very next day. I quit the job after New Year and I've never been back to the place. I don't know, I just felt it was better not to go near there, kind of like a premonition."

She toyed with a paper coaster, lost in her thoughts. "Sometimes I get the feeling that everything that happened to me on my twentieth birthday was some kind of illusion. It's as though something happened to make me think that things happened that never really happened at all. But I know for sure that they *did* happen. I can still bring back vivid images of every piece of furniture and every nick-nack in room 604. What happened to me in there really happened, and it had an important meaning for me, too."

The two of us remained silent, drinking our drinks and thinking our separate thoughts.

"Do you mind if I ask you one thing?" I asked. "Or, more precisely, two things."

"Go ahead," she said. "I imagine you're going to ask me what I wished for that time. That's the first thing you want to know."

"But it seems as though you don't want to talk about it."

"Does it?"

I nodded.

She put the coaster down and narrowed her eyes as though staring at something off in the distance. "You're not supposed to tell anybody what you wish for, you know."

"I won't try to drag it out of you," I said. "I would like to know whether or not it came true, though. And also – whatever the wish itself might have been – whether or not you later came to regret what it was you chose to wish for. Were you ever sorry you didn't wish for something else?"

"The answer to the first question is 'yes' and also 'no'. I still have a lot of living left to do, probably. I haven't seen how things are going to work out in the end."

"So it was a wish that takes time to come true?"

"You could say that. Time is going to play an important rôle."

"Like in cooking?"

"Like in cooking."

I thought about that for a moment, but the only thing that came to mind was the image of a gigantic pie slowly cooking in an oven at low heat.

"And the answer to my second question?"

"What was that again?"

"Whether you ever regretted your choice of what to wish for."

A moment of silence followed. The eyes she turned on me seemed to lack any depth. The desiccated shadow of a smile flickered at the corners of her mouth, suggesting a kind of hushed sense of resignation.

"I'm married now," she said. "To an accountant three years my senior. And I have two children, a boy and a girl. We have an Irish setter. I drive an Audi and I play tennis with my friends twice a week. That's the life I'm living now."

"Sounds pretty good to me," I said.

"Even if the Audi's bumper has two dents in it?"

"Hey, bumpers are *made* for denting."

"That would make a great bumper sticker," she said. " 'Bumpers are for denting'."

I looked at her mouth as she said that.

"What I'm trying to tell you is this," she said, more softly, scratching an earlobe. It was a beautifully-shaped earlobe. "No matter what they wish for, no matter how far they go, people can never be anything but themselves. That's all."

"There's another good bumper sticker," I said. " 'No matter how far you go, you can never be anything but yourself'."

She laughed aloud, with a real show of pleasure, and the shadow was gone.

She rested her elbow on the bar and looked at me. "Tell me," she said. "What would you have wished for if you had been in my position?"

"On the night of my twentieth birthday, you mean?"

"Uh-huh."

I took some time to think about that, but I couldn't come up with an answer.

"I can't think of anything," I confessed. "I'm too far away now from my twentieth birthday."

"You really can't think of anything?"

I shook my head.

"Not one thing?"

"Not one thing."

She looked into my eyes again – straight in – and said, "That's because you've already made your wish."

*

"But you had better think about it very carefully because I can grant you only one." In the darkness somewhere, an old man wearing a withered-leaf-coloured tie raises a finger. "Just one. You can't change your mind afterwards and take it back."

Acknowledgements

"My Birthday, Your Birthday" and author introductions
translated from the Japanese by Jay Rubin: © Jay Rubin, 2004

"The Moor" in *The Angel on the Roof* by Russell Banks:
© Russell Banks, 2000. Reprinted by permission of Ellen Levine
Literary Agency/Trident Media Group

"Dundun" in *Jesus' Son* by Denis Johnson:
© Denis Johnson, 1992.
Published by agreement with Methuen Publishing Ltd

"Timothy's Birthday" in *After Rain* by William Trevor:
© William Trevor, 1993

"The Birthday Cake" in *The Last Good Man* by Daniel Lyons:
© Daniel Lyons, 1993

"Turning" by Lynda Sexson in *Hamlet's Planets: Parables*:
© Lynda Sexson, 1996

"Forever Overhead" by David Foster Wallace in the collection
Brief Interviews with Hideous Men published by Little Brown &
Co, used by permission of the Author:
© David Foster Wallace, 1999

"Angel of Mercy, Angel of Wrath" by Ethan Canin
First Published in *Boston Globe*, 1989: © Ethan Canin, 1989

"The Birthday Present" in *Interesting Women* by Andrea Lee:
© Andrea Lee, 2002. Reprinted by permission of HarperCollins
Publishers Ltd

www.randomhouse.co.uk/vintage